DEATH IN THE LOUVRE

A Paris Booksellers Mystery

EVAN HIRST

Copyright

Death in the Louvre is a work of fiction. Names, characters, organizations, places, events, and incidents are either products of the author's imagination or are used fictitiously.

ABOUT THE AUTHOR

Spurred on by a passion for history and a love of adventure, Evan Hirst is an award-winning screen writer who has lived and worked all over the world and now lives in Paris.

Evan's *Paris Booksellers Mysteries* are light-hearted cozy mysteries that plunge you into the joys and tribulations of living in Paris, where food, wine and crime make life worth living... along with a book or two.

Evan also writes the *Isa Floris* thrillers that blend together far-flung locations, ancient mysteries and fast-paced action in an intriguing mix of fact and fiction aimed at keeping you on the edge of your seat.

Find out more about Evan Hirst's books at

www.evanhirst.com

CHAPTER 1

The sky over Paris was a pale shade of grey. It was a pearl grey with large swathes of pink and yellow splashed through it. The early morning June sky promised a warm sunny afternoon. For the moment, cotton-candy clouds drifted peacefully across it. The clouds moved so slowly that the sun played hide and seek with them: popping out in a glorious beam of light only to disappear behind the next fluffy mass.

When bright rays of sunshine came pouring into the Café Mollien in the Denon Wing of the Louvre Museum, Ava Sext was in heaven. Seated at an alcove table directly in front of a huge antique window that gave onto the Carrousel Garden across the road, she watched the sunlight dance on *Arc de Triomphe* at the garden's entrance. The gold leaf on its statues glittered in the bright light just as it must have two

1

hundred years earlier when the arch was built to commemorate Napoleon Bonaparte's military victories

Like a cat basking in the sun, Ava leaned back in the warm sunshine. Two hundred years ago, who could have imagined that she -- Ava Sext, born and raised in London -- would one day be enjoying the scene over a late breakfast? And that she would be enjoying it as a Parisian...

Ava pushed her long brown hair behind her ears. Dressed in loose-fit jeans and a chic blue top by an Italian designer, she had a magenta-colored leopard print chiffon scarf jauntily wrapped around her neck, fuchsia pink sports shoes on her feet and a touch of bright red lipstick on her lips. The rest of her heart-shaped face was makeup free. Anyone looking at her would think she was French.

"Cappuccino, a double espresso, cheesecake and an apple tart," a tall man said, setting a tray down on the table in front of her.

With a smile, Ava looked up at Henri DeAth who was looking especially dapper that morning. He was wearing dark jeans and a pale blue shirt that made his blue eyes look even bluer. A charcoal grey sweater was thrown over his shoulders. Salt and pepper hair curled around his face like a halo. In his sixties, Henri had the youngest spirit of anyone she had ever met.

Henri had been a friend of Ava's late Uncle Charles.

After an inheritance, Charles Sext, a New Scotland Yard detective, had quit his job and moved to France to run an outdoor book stand on a Parisian quay overlooking the Seine River, having decided to enjoy life far from crime and criminals. However, sleuthing was in his blood. Before his death last year, he and Henri had solved several crimes together that had brought them some renown.

"A sunny day. A perfect day to visit the Louvre," Henri announced. "What tourist in his right mind would want to spend such a glorious day in a dusty museum?"

Having seen hundreds of people lined up at the pyramid entrance to the Louvre, Ava knew there were quite a few.

As Henri slid into the seat across from her, Ava, hungrier than she would like to admit, removed the items from the tray and spread them across the table.

"What do you want?" she asked, trying to keep her gaze off the apple tart that was screaming her name. The cappuccino was also calling out to her.

"Ladies' choice," Henri replied, always the gentleman.

"You go first," Ava said, hoping that he would ask for the cheesecake.

Henri raised his eyebrows. With an amused smile, he pointed at the tart and the cappuccino. Ava's heart sank.

"Those are for you. But if you prefer the cheesecake and espresso, I'll be happy to change," Henri said.

"No. I accept my fate," Ava replied with a grateful grin. She pulled the apple tart and cappuccino toward her before he changed his mind.

Henri rolled his eyes over the café's soaring ceilings, massive stone pillars and the ornate monumental staircase that led up to the café from the ground floor. "This is quite a change from Café Zola."

Café Zola was on the *Quai Malaquais* on the left bank of the Seine River in the center of Paris. Across the street from his book stand, the café was Henri's daily coffee and lunch spot. It was a traditional café where the waiters wore long white aprons over their dark trousers and were known to be grumpy on occasion. If Ava were honest, they were grumpy on a daily basis. But that was part of Café Zola's charm.

"When are Gerard and Alain going to reopen?" Ava asked, trying to hide the worry in her voice. Gerard and Alain were the two cousins who owned Café Zola. Gerard dealt with the customers while Alain spent his time in the café's tiny kitchen, whipping up unforgettable meals. The café had closed for works after a water leak.

"In two weeks. They've decided to renovate," Henri answered, taking a sip of his espresso.

"Renovate!" Ava repeated, horrified. "You mean modernize?" Images of neon lights and brightly-colored hip furnishings appeared before her eyes.

"Gerard and Alain? Modernize... Never. They don't even know what the word means. They're just "freshening up" the decor."

Ava furrowed her brow, not at all reassured by the term "freshening up".

Henri gestured at Café Mollien's lavish ornamentation. "This is an opportunity to spend time in the Louvre. We see it every day from our book stands, but I can't remember the last time I was here. Until Café Zola reopens, we can have breakfast here and see some art at the same time."

"That leaves lunch," Ava said, taking a bite of her tart. It melted in her mouth. Its sweet crust contrasted perfectly with the apples' tartness.

Watching her, Henri burst out laughing. "For a skinny English girl who arrived last year, you've turned into quite the French gourmet."

"That's your fault and Alain's," Ava replied, content.

The first time Ava had gone to Café Zola, she had ordered a sandwich for lunch. Alain was so upset that he marched out of the kitchen to see what was wrong. The sandwich was quickly replaced by a *coq au vin*, rooster in wine sauce, and a *tarte tatin*, a caramelized upside down apple tart, for dessert. It was delicious. It was also life-changing. Ava's sandwich days were behind her.

Gazing blissfully at her surroundings, Ava smiled. "I

never thought I'd go to work and see the Louvre every day. In London, my office looked on a brick wall with dripping blood painted on it."

Thinking back to her career in London, Ava shuddered. A communication specialist in a boutique PR firm, her days and nights had been devoted to posting social media posts and tweeting for her celebrity clients. She realized it was time to leave when she had gone on a drunken tweeting frenzy after a romantic relationship had ended badly, and no one had noticed. In fact, some clients had even complimented her on the originality of her tweets!

Seeing the expression on her face, Henri misread her thoughts. He nodded as he bit into his cheesecake. "I agree. These pastries don't hold a candle to Alain's desserts, but we have to eat."

Ava took a sip of her cappuccino and studied the mass of humanity that was hurrying up the staircase to the Grand Gallery. People rushed by without breaking pace. Since she and Henri had arrived, the crowds coming up the stairs had grown denser.

"Where are they all going?" Ava asked, curious.

"To see the Louvre's most famous lady… the Mona Lisa. I'm afraid the only thing they'll be able on a day like today is the head of the person in front of them. If you want to visit the Mona Lisa, you need to come on a winter evening. You'll be alone with her."

For a brief instant, Ava almost wished it were winter so she could experience that intimacy. But the sunlight streaming through the window changed her mind. It was summer. If she had her way, the beautiful weather would last forever.

"When did you last see the Mona Lisa?" Henri asked.

"I can't remember." No sooner had the words escaped her lips than a school trip to the Louvre years ago came to mind. At the time, Ava, who must have been fourteen, had been more interested in a boy called Jason than in art. She had a vague memory of standing in front of the Mona Lisa as he chatted up another girl, breaking Ava's heart.

"The Mona Lisa is a wonderful painting, but it's far from my favorite," Henri said.

"What are we seeing today?" Ava asked, taking another forkful of her apple tart. She was so ravenous, she considered picking it up with her fingers and biting into it. She refrained from doing so. Certain things were not done in France.

"13th and 14th century Italian painting," Henri said. "We'll see works by Lorenzo Monaco, Bartolo di Fredi and Pisanello. Pisanello's portrait of the Princess of Este is enchanting." Gazing at the mass of people walking up the staircase, he shook his head. "Don't worry. We'll be far from the madding crowd."

"I remember visiting museums on school trips. We were shepherded past painting after painting without having the chance to look at any of them. Angels and saints, sinners and sinking ships... they all blended into one big blur," Ava said, twirling her fork in the air.

Henri grinned. "I prefer sinners. Saints are never much fun."

"Uncle Charles would have agreed with you. He liked rogues and villains. I think he'd be disappointed in me."

Henri burst out laughing. "You're still young. There's plenty of time to pick up vices."

Finding his words encouraging, Ava finished her tart. "Cheesecake and apple tart aren't very French for breakfast."

"All the better. If you believed the clichés, I'd have a beret on my head, and you'd have bright pink hair. Besides, this is a late breakfast. It doesn't follow the normal Parisian breakfast rules."

Ava studied Henri as he drank his espresso. He was at home in the ostentatious gold and marble surroundings. Henri was a former French *notaire*, a notary. In France, a notary was a member of a powerful caste. They were wealthy, secretive and protective of privileges that went back hundreds of years.

Henri had once joked to Ava, "Not only do we know where the bodies are buried, we buried them... if we didn't kill the people ourselves."

A French notary giving up his practice before he was in his dotage or dead was a rare as Christmas in August...

Impossible.

However, Henri was Christmas in August.

And also in May, June and July.

In short, Henri was an unusual man.

He had come to Paris from Bordeaux -- a city in southwestern France, hub of the Bordeaux wine-growing region -- to deal with a tricky inheritance. Her Uncle Charles's apartment where she now lived had sprung from that, as had the book stands and Henri's country house in the middle of Paris.

At a mere sixty, Henri had sold his practice to his nephew and moved to Paris. Henri's former clients still appeared on a regular basis to ask him for advice. But after a long leisurely lunch at Café Zola, they would leave, reassured.

To Ava, it seemed that if anyone lived life fully, it was Henri. He truly enjoyed people. He loved food, knowledge and beauty. He had a great sense of humor and had been a true friend to her since she had moved to Paris to become a bookseller.

And after they had saved Yves Dubois, a university professor, from being murdered, she and Henri were now partners in sleuthing.

"*Sext and DeAth*. It has a nice ring to it, doesn't it?" Ava asked.

"Are you having a sign made?" Henri asked, smiling.

"Of course not. I just find it curious that you and my uncle became friends. Knowing him, he would have found the wordplay on your names extremely funny."

Henri grinned. "I agree. Charles liked the ring of *Sext and DeAth*."

Ava nodded. Henri's last name was often a source of astonishment for English speakers. DeAth was an old Flemish name. *De* meant from. *Ath* was a city in Belgium. Over time, the pronunciation of the last name had come to rhyme with the English word "death". As both her uncle and Henri possessed a wicked sense of humor, Ava suspected their last names had made their friendship inevitable.

Thinking of her uncle, Ava glanced away to hide the tears in her eyes. She owed her Paris life to him. In his will, he had left her an apartment and money. More importantly, he had left her Henri.

Looking around, Ava noticed that the café was now half-full.

When had everyone snuck in?

When she and Henri had arrived, the café had been empty.

Her Uncle Charles had often said that people miss half

10

their lives because they don't see what's going on around them. Ava might not have missed half her life, but she had certainly missed the last ten minutes.

All at once, a shadow loomed over her.

A tall man in his late forties with wavy brown hair and blue eyes, even bluer than Henri's eyes, was standing next to her. He seemed relieved to see her. As his eyes ran over her face, his expression changed. Confused, he looked up and peered out the window.

Startled, Ava eyed the man, waiting. French people didn't walk up to strangers unless it was urgent.

"It's a beautiful day, isn't it?" the man asked in a posh English accent.

The moment Ava heard his accent, she smiled. The man was not a desperate Frenchman. He was a fellow compatriot who had fallen under the city's spell.

"June is a lovely month to visit Paris," Henri said.

The man eyed Henri. "Do we know one another?"

"I don't believe so. I'm Henri DeAth." Henri gestured at Ava. "My friend is Ava Sext."

The man smiled. "I'm George Starr."

"Are you here on a visit?" Henri asked in a breezy tone.

"No. I'm lucky enough to live here," George said with a grin. He turned his head to the right. Instantly, his body became rigid. Turning white, he stepped back as if warding off a blow.

Noticing the dramatic change in the man's behavior, Ava glanced around to see what had caused it. All she saw was a sea of shouting French schoolchildren being corralled through the café to the outside terrace by their teachers.

And then, like in a film, everything happened at once.

Or so it seemed to Ava.

George tilted forward and fell over the table. "Sorry. How clumsy of me," he said as he pulled himself up, clutching the chair next to her.

Before Ava could respond, George turned and sprinted out of the café, pushing his way through the rambunctious children.

Alarmed, Ava jumped up. "Henri! Something's wrong!"

Having sensed that something was off, Henri was already on his feet.

"He's headed to the stairs, Henri!" Ava shouted as she ran to the black and gold wrought iron railing that overlooked the stairway. When she reached it, there was a loud, ear-shattering scream.

The scream echoed through the café.

In horror, Ava glanced down and saw George Starr fly up in the air and go bouncing down the stone stairs. His body hit the landing with a loud thud.

For a moment, time stopped.

Everyone was silent.

No one moved.

Then sheer chaos ensued.

Screams and shouts of horror rang up from the stairwell.

Ava started to run toward the stairs. Henri held her back.

The screams and shouts were now coming from all around them. Everyone in the café leapt up and ran to the railing to see what had happened.

Feeling sick, Ava pressed her back against a stone pillar and looked down at George. His body was sprawled on the stone landing. His head was at an odd angle, and blood dripped from the back of his skull. There was no question of whether he was dead or alive.

No one could have survived a fall like that.

With a solemn look on his face, Henri turned to Ava. "I suggest we postpone our museum visit."

Frozen to the spot, Ava stared down at the body of the man who had been chatting gaily with her seconds before.

In a flash, Ava knew that the death was not an accident. For some unknown reason, George Starr had been murdered. Looking down at his lifeless body, Ava vowed to discover who the murderer was.

CHAPTER 2

Clutching the gold and black iron railing in the Café Denon, Ava took one deep breath after another. Everything around her was spinning in circles. She leaned against the massive stone pillar next to her, unable to take her eyes off George Starr's dead body, sprawled on the marble landing below.

Ava felt a gentle tug on her arm.

"It's time to go," Henri said softly.

She swallowed and looked up. Tears were in her eyes. "Do you think George suffered?"

Henri shook his head. "No. He probably died instantly."

"It's strange. I just met George, but I feel like a friend has died," Ava said in a near whisper.

Henri shook his head in agreement. "His death was unfortunate."

"Unfortunate? It was awful," Ava said, incensed. People always spoke about the English having a stiff upper lip, but the French were masters of avoiding emotion in stressful situations.

"It was a tragedy," Henri conceded.

"Henri, it's not normal that someone you've just met dies five minutes later. In fact, it's odd... Do you really think it was an accident?" Ava asked.

Henri looked down at George's body. He sighed and pursed his lips. "Accidents happen. People fall and die. It's part of life. Not every death is a murder."

But some are, Ava thought.

"It's time to go," Henri insisted.

Forging a path through the crowd of people who were pushing forward to see the body, Henri and Ava moved away from the railing. When they reached their table, Ava sank down into her chair, shell-shocked.

"What's going to happen now?"

"The authorities will check the security footage to see if there was anything odd about his fall. After that, they'll contact his next of kin."

Ava was silent. Looking up, she could almost see George Starr standing next to her. With a sigh, she finished her cappuccino.

Henri eyed a cloth bag that was hanging on a chair next

to her. "You shouldn't leave your belongings unattended."

"There's only a sketchbook and some drawing materials in it," Ava said. "Nothing worth taking."

"A gift from Ali?" Henri asked.

Ava nodded.

Ali Beltran ran the book stand next to hers with his twin brother, Hassan. Ali was a prize-winning painter who had graduated from the prestigious Paris school of arts, the *Beaux Arts* Academy. He often sketched at his stand. In an effort to get Ava to draw, he had given her a sketchbook.

"Ali would turn everyone into an artist if he could," Henri added, in an attempt to lighten the atmosphere.

"Ali says that drawing improves your observational skills."

"Observation is the key to many things," Henri replied.

Ava glanced out the window. The Arc de Triomphe looked exactly as it had before George's death. Hundreds of smiling tourists continued to take pictures of it, unaware that someone had died in the Louvre.

"Ready to leave?" Henri asked.

"Ready!" Ava said. She stood up and slung the cloth bag over her shoulder. *Et la vie continue*, she thought... Life goes on.

Henri pushed his way through the excited throng inside the Café. Ava followed him. When they reached the exit, it was closed. A security guard was preventing people from entering.

Seeing Henri and Ava, he moved aside to let them leave.

They stepped out of the café. They were now standing directly at the top of the stairs. Ava glanced down at the landing. Medics and security guards surrounded George's body.

A medical crew carrying a stretcher ran up the stairs from the ground floor.

It's too late for that, Ava thought.

Ava and Henri strode past the guards who were pushing the crowd back with outstretched arms. They stopped at the entrance of the Denon Wing's main gallery. Henri walked up to a guard who was wearing an earpiece that crackled loudly.

"What's the best way out?" Henri asked.

The guard looked up. "Go straight through the Grand Gallery and down the stairs. From there, follow the signs," he said as sweat ran down his forehead.

Henri and Ava entered the Grand Gallery. While Henri walked quickly, Ava had trouble keeping up with him. She wanted to sink to the ground and weep. She forced herself to soldier on.

Suddenly, there was a loud piercing scream from the area near the stairway.

Alarmed, Ava turned. At first, all she saw was the crowd

pushing forward. Then a thin woman with long dark hair and a heart-shaped face ran toward her, knocking into everyone. The woman's face was pale, and she was trembling. When she brushed past Ava, their grief-stricken eyes met for the briefest of moments. Then the woman was gone.

She vanished so quickly that Ava wondered if she hadn't imagined her.

Henri was now standing next to Ava. "Are you OK?"

"Did you see the woman?"

Henri knitted his eyebrows. "No. I heard a scream and came back. What did she look like?"

"Sad," Ava said. "Sad!"

Henri took Ava's arm and steered her through the crowd. Ava's mind was lost in a thick fog.

She had met George Starr, a compatriot, and now he was dead... murdered in the Louvre! Things like that don't happen in real life!

After a few more steps, Ava made a beeline for a wooden bench in the middle of the gallery. She sank down onto it. "I'm going to be sick," she told Henri.

"You've had a shock," he said, sitting down next to her.

Ava put her head between her legs and took several deep breaths. After a few seconds, she looked up.

"Feeling better?" Henri asked, handing her a linen handkerchief.

With tears running down her face, she nodded. She

gripped the handkerchief like a buoy.

"We're in no rush," Henri said, eyeing her with concern.

"Give me a minute." Ava closed her eyes. Instead of darkness, she saw George's lifeless body. Shaken, she opened her eyes and jumped up. "I want to go back to my stand."

"You don't want to rest some more?" Henri asked, worried.

"No," Ava said.

They began to walk. Ava looked at the gallery. Gigantic historical paintings by French artists covered the walls from floor to ceiling. Each painting seemed to vie with the others for the number of bodies it contained. Whether it was on the battlefield, at city walls or on a shipwrecked raft, the vacant look of death stared out at Ava. And in each painting, she saw George Starr.

Henri and Ava skirted around the gift shop and entered the next room. Ava was relieved to see portraits instead of paintings of death and destruction. But even in the portraits, the eyes of the sitter seemed aware of their mortality.

Henri halted in front of an unfinished painting on an easel. It was a copy of a larger painting hanging on the wall. The copy was much smaller than the original. A palette of oil paints was on a small folding stool next to the easel. The artist wasn't there.

Ava glanced at the original on the wall. It was a painting of the young shepherd Endymion by Anne-Louis Girodet. As Ava studied the handsome shepherd who had fallen into an eternal sleep, a shiver ran through her. She then glanced at the copy. The person copying the painting had captured the stillness of death.

When a security guard saw them near the canvas, he walked up and hovered nearby.

Henri turned to Ava. "A painter's education used to start by copying paintings. It's a method that's fallen out of favor."

Ava frowned. She couldn't understand why Henri had chosen this moment to give her a lecture on art education.

"Henri. Is this really the time to be looking at art?" Ava asked.

"It is if the painter is George Starr," Henri replied as he continued to examine the canvas on the easel.

Ava reeled backwards, stunned. "George Starr painted this?"

"George had some titanium dioxide paint on his hand when he spoke to us. If I'm not mistaken, that's the same white we can see there," Henri said, pointing at some paint near the shepherd's eyes.

Ava looked from the painting to Henri and back again. She was amazed. "You noticed paint on George's hand?"

Henri nodded. "It's a habit I picked up as a notary.

People are usually very bad at explaining themselves. However, if you watch and study them closely, you can learn a lot."

Knowing that George might have painted the unfinished artwork changed everything. Suddenly, Ava's attention was focused on the canvas. Perhaps the clue to George's untimely death lay in front of her. While George's painting was much smaller than the original, it captured the original's tragic force. In some ways, George's painting was even more tragic.

"If George did paint this, he was incredibly talented," Ava said.

"Copyists at the Louvre are very talented," Henri replied.

Ava walked over to the guard. "Is the painter coming back soon?"

"He said he'd be back in twenty minutes," the guard replied.

Ava didn't tell have the heart to tell him that the painter would not be coming back.

Feeling an overwhelming sense of injustice that George would never finish his painting, Ava walked over to Henri. "It's time to leave. There's nothing more we can do here."

After one last glance at George's painting, Henri and Ava headed to massive stone staircase at the gallery's far end. Ava gripped the railing as she went down the steps. Several times, she felt dizzy and wanted to stop. She forced herself to continue.

The faster they left the Louvre, the better.

On the ground floor, Henri led Ava through a warren of rooms toward the museum exit. As they walked, the angels, saints and sinners hanging on the walls blurred together in Ava's mind.

She wondered if George was a saint or a sinner.

Not that the two were mutually exclusive.

You might be a saint in one area and a sinner in another.

From her brief time with George, Ava guessed that he had been more of a sinner than a saint.

When Ava and Henri reached the atrium under the glass pyramid, sunlight was streaming down into it as fluffy clouds floated in the blue sky overhead.

Everything was as it should be... except that it wasn't.

George Starr was dead.

He would never finish his painting.

And Ava would never have the opportunity to speak with him again.

Leaving the museum, Ava stared at the flashing red lights of the police and fire department vehicles that were parked in front of the emergency exit of the Denon Wing. She choked back a sob.

The strident wail of an ambulance's siren as it roared off

with its lights flashing drowned out the chatter of the crowds who were waiting in line to enter the museum.

Henri and Ava walked in silence.

When they neared the windows of the Café Mollien, Ava looked up at the window where she had met George Starr.

Suddenly, she stopped dead in her tracks.

Clenching her jaw, she whirled toward Henri. "Henri, something is rotten in Denmark."

Puzzled, he slowed and stared at her. "That's from *Hamlet* by Shakespeare. Wasn't that what the officer said when the king's ghost appeared?"

Ava nodded. "Yes. But in our case, something is rotten in the Denon Wing of the Louvre. We need to discover what that is."

A worried look spread across Henri's face.

CHAPTER 3

Sitting in the shade of a tall tree in her green and white lawn chair, Ava looked up at the sky. The clouds had vanished, leaving a blue sky and a brightly shining sun. On the Quai Malaquais where she and Henri had their book stands, Parisians and tourists were out in droves. Some were strolling at a leisurely pace. Others on skateboards zigzagged in and out of the crowd. Still others rode their *Velib'* share bikes, ringing the bikes' tinny bells when people got in their way.

Up and down the quay, book lovers were browsing through the used books in the stands in search of a hidden gem. Unless you considered a 1998 Baedeker Guide to Egypt or a handwritten sandwich cookbook a treasure, anyone looking through Ava's stand would be sadly disappointed.

Glancing at the joyful people around her, it was clear that no one was aware that George Starr had been murdered in the Louvre.

With a sigh, Ava glanced over at Henri's stand. It was shuttered. When they had returned from the Louvre, a formally dressed couple in their eighties had been waiting for Henri. Ava had instantly identified them as his former clients. The worried expressions on their faces and the thick file that the man clutched in his hand were signs that only Henri could help them.

Henri's nephew, who now ran the notarial office, had grown used to his clients coming to Paris to obtain Henri's advice. Fortunately, he wasn't the least bit offended by it. He had even joked that his clients got two notaries for the price of one. As Café Zola was closed, Henri had taken the couple to a restaurant on the rue Bonaparte for lunch. Ava knew from experience that a meeting like that might last hours.

Restless, she rose from her chair and strode over to her stand -- the 8.60 meters of bottle-green wooden boxes that were perched on a stone wall overlooking the Seine River.

In an attempt to chase away her blues, she eyed the license taped inside the first green box. The license was written in French. It had several official stamps and seals on it. It stated that Ava Sext was granted the right to run the stand by the city of Paris.

Ava was a "*bouquinist*" -- a bookseller that sold used books out of the green boxes that lined the Seine River in the center of Paris. Since 1859, concessions to the green boxes that ran from the Pont Marie to the Quai de Louvre and from the Quai de la Tournelle to the Quai Voltaire had been granted by the city of Paris to a lucky few.

Ava was one of them.

For her, her stand was paradise. But today, there was trouble in paradise.

Looking up at the Louvre on the other side of the Seine, she relived the moment George Starr had come up to her table. For a few brief minutes, he had spoken with her, alive and smiling. Then something or someone had frightened him. He had fled and had fallen to his death.

Ava frowned.

Oddly, she didn't remember anyone looking at George or running through the café after him.

Still, it would be obvious to anyone vaguely observant that George Starr's death had been a murder.

Ava didn't know who had killed him or why... But clearly someone had murdered him. People just don't fall down stairs and die.

She sighed.

In some ways, Henri was right: people do fall down stairs and die.

However, Ava had never had someone speak to her and die a tragic death seconds later. It had to be a murder!

An unsettling thought popped into her mind.

Maybe George wasn't the unlucky one.

Maybe she was the unlucky one.

This was her second dead man in two months. Although her first dead man was alive and well, thanks to Sext and DeAth.

Ava felt sad. George Starr was dead and would stay dead. There was nothing that she and Henri could do now but find his murderer.

First, she had to convince Henri that George Starr had been murdered.

She hadn't explicitly stated her suspicions on that matter to Henri. He would have said that she was jumping to conclusions.

Well, a man was dead!

Someone had to do a little jumping, or the murder would never be solved.

Looking sideways, she saw that Hassan Beltran had just arrived at his stand. Hassan, a good-looking man in his early-thirties with a shock of thick brown hair, had a wicked sense of humor like his twin brother, Ali. Although the brothers looked alike, they were as different as chalk and cheese. Ali never knew what Ava was thinking, while Hassan always did.

Wandering over from his stand, Hassan showed Ava a porcelain shepherdess with one lone sheep. "What do you think?"

"It needs another sheep," Ava said with a frown.

Hassan appeared offended. While Ali was a painter, Hassan was a lover of objects. When Hassan wasn't on the quay, he traveled all across Europe looking for objects. The curios Ava sold in her stand were some of Hassan's minor finds.

Hassan narrowed his eyes and stared at Ava. "Is something wrong?"

"I thought you'd never ask," she said, anxious to talk. "I saw a man murdered today!"

Confused, Hassan eyed Ava as if she had been sitting in the sun too long. "Didn't you and Henri go to the Louvre this morning?"

"We did. We were having coffee at Café Mollien, and then it happened…" Ava said, sweeping her arms out dramatically.

"Could you define what "*and then it happened*" means?" Hassan asked, frowning.

"A tall Englishman with blue eyes, even bluer than Henri's eyes, came up to our table. His name was George Starr."

Hassan rubbed his nose as he often did when he was

concentrating. "George Starr? Was he a friend of yours?"

"George Starr? No. I just met him this morning."

Silent, Hassan waited for her to continue her tale.

"We were talking about the weather... Then he was dead."

"George Starr?"

"Yes," Ava said.

"Someone shot him in front of you?" Hassan questioned.

"No," Ava snapped.

Hassan raised his eyebrows. "He was stabbed by a madman driven crazy by the crowds?"

Ava shook her head, annoyed that Hassan was not taking her seriously. "In the Louvre? Of course not. If George had been shot or stabbed, everyone would know it was a murder. Instead, what happened was even more diabolical."

Baffled, Hassan waited patiently for her explanation as he shifted the shepherdess from hand to hand.

For the first time, Ava realized that to anyone who hadn't been there, the death might appear to be an accident. A ripple of indignation ran through her.

George's death was a murder!

She knew a murder when she saw one.

Not that she had ever seen one. But she had almost been shot on her last case, and that counted for something.

"I'm waiting," Hassan said as he placed the shepherdess

in Ava's stand.

Ava took a deep breath. "Henri and I were in the Café Mollien. George Starr walked over to our table and spoke to us."

Hassan frowned. "And you didn't know him?"

"He was English," Ava explained.

"That makes sense," Hassan said.

Ava didn't quite know what Hassan meant by that remark. Undeterred, she continued her explanation. "George was talking to us. Suddenly, he turned, ran out of the café and dashed down the steps."

"The monumental double staircase?" Hassan asked.

"The very same," Ava said. "The stairs were packed with people."

"On their way to see the Mona Lisa…"

Ava wanted to crown Hassan. How could she tell the story when he kept interrupting her? "Yes, on their way to see the Mona Lisa. George went hurtling down the steps and hit his head."

"*Oh là là!* Dead?" Hassan said with a stricken look on his face.

"Dead," Ava confirmed with a solemn nod, glad that Hassan was finally acknowledging the gravity of the situation.

"Did you see who pushed him?" Hassan asked.

"No," Ava said.

"Then why couldn't it have been an accident?" Hassan asked, rubbing his nose again.

"Because George ran out of the café like the devil was on his tail!" Ava said, paraphrasing a French expression.

"Maybe he was late for an appointment," Hassan suggested. "What does Henri think?"

"We haven't spoken about it," Ava confessed.

Hassan's expression changed instantly. *Case Closed* was written all over his face.

"Just because Henri needs to be hit over the head with a hammer before he admits a murder is a murder doesn't mean I don't know a murder when I see one," Ava protested. "If only I could learn more, I know I could convince Henri."

"That's no problem," Hassan replied.

"How are we going to find out what happened? We can't very well call up the police and ask them," Ava replied sharply.

Hassan raised his eyebrows and smiled. "Claude Monet will tell us."

"Monet, the impressionist painter? He's been dead for one hundred years."

"Not that Claude Monet, my Claude Monet. He's a client."

Too late, Ava remembered that Hassan knew every collector in Paris. Whenever he was at his stand, people would wander by nonstop to see what treasures he had found and to tell him what they needed for their collections.

"Claude is with the police?" Ava asked, bright-eyed.

With a disapproving shake of his head, Hassan stared at Ava. "The French police are the soul of secrecy. Of course, he's not with the police. Claude's the head of security at the Louvre."

Ava could feel her excitement growing. "Can I talk to him?"

"Slow down. I'll see if I can convince him to come by for a few minutes. Fortunately for you, I found a glass paperweight he wants for his collection. I'll get him to come here. He and I will chat. I'll lead him onto this morning's unfortunate incident, and we'll see where that leads."

Without waiting for her response, Hassan pulled his cell phone out of his pocket and dialed a number. Ava was so happy that she almost danced a jig.

"Claude. It's Hassan, Hassan Beltran. I found the paperweight you wanted. I'm at the stand. Can you come by?" Hassan asked. He listened, nodding. "I understand. You're busy now..."

Ava was disappointed. Of course, Claude Monet couldn't come. After all, there had just been a murder in the Louvre.

"Thirty minutes. Perfect," Hassan said and hung up.

"He's coming?" Ava asked, incredulous.

In detective novels, you don't ask for information and have it fall in your lap.

That was called a *Deus Ex Machina*...

A *Deus Ex Machina* – God in the Machine -- was the God that came down from the heavens in ancient Greek and Roman plays to tell you who did it and why. In detective novels, it was highly frowned upon to have this happen.

But this wasn't a detective novel.

This was real life.

Who would have imagined that a *Deus Ex Machina* would appear when Ava needed one? Or that it would come in the form of a *Claude Monet Ex Machina,* to be more precise?

"Do you want the shepherdess or not?" Hassan asked pointing at the statue.

"I'll take her," Ava replied, knowing that Hassan would be vexed if she didn't say yes.

A contented smile appeared on his face. "She's a beauty. Someone will buy her before the afternoon's out."

"Shouldn't Claude be investigating the death?" Ava asked, perplexed.

"The police investigate. Claude is probably up to his neck in paperwork on the accident. He'll be glad to take a break."

"We don't know it was an accident," Ava countered.

"If it were murder, Claude wouldn't be able to pull

himself away from the office," Hassan replied.

Ava nodded. She remained silent. There was certain logic to what Hassan had just said. However, just because it was logical didn't mean it was right. George Starr's death was a murder, and she intended to prove it.

Hassan eyed the determined look in her eyes, uneasy. "I'll wave you over when I'm ready for you."

Thirty minutes later, an impeccably groomed man in his fifties, wearing a well-cut suit and a crisp white shirt whose top button was unbuttoned, walked up to Hassan's stand. The only sign that the man worked in the Louvre was the crepe soles on his shoes. Anyone who worked there would have to walk miles of corridors each day.

From a distance, Ava watched the men talk. Their conversation was lively. There were lots of French hand gestures and nods. After a few minutes, Hassan turned and signaled to Ava to come join them.

Trying to remain calm, she strolled over to the men slowly, ordering her heart to beat slower.

When she reached them, Claude Monet ran his eyes over her in a very professional manner that made her feel uneasy. If she had been a crook, Claude Monet would have had her confessing in minutes. At the same time, there was something about the man that made her trust him.

Hassan put his hand on Ava's shoulder and introduced her. "Ava has come to us from London. She's taken over her late Uncle Charles's stand."

A look of recognition spread across Claude's face. "I'm sorry for your loss. Charlie was a wonderful man. He was a true professional. We often spoke about his time at New Scotland Yard."

"I'm lucky he was my uncle. He was unique," Ava replied with a smile.

"And now you've taken over from him?" Claude asked, balancing back on his heels as his eyes drilled into her.

Ava didn't know if Claude Monet knew about her sleuthing with Henri. She decided to avoid that aspect of the question. Parsing her words, Ava responded. "Yes, I've taken over his stand. My uncle wanted me to love Paris as he did."

Hassan jumped into the conversation. "Ava and Henri were having coffee at Café Mollien this morning when the unfortunate accident occurred. Ava is quite shaken."

Claude eyed her with compassion. "It's never easy to see someone lose their life."

"Did you find out what happened?" Ava asked quickly, a bit too quickly as she could tell from Claude's sharp-eyed frown.

"The man fell and died. He was unlucky. It was unfortunate that it happened on one of the museum's busiest days. But *c'est la vie.* That's life. We're all sad that George Starr, a member of the Louvre family, died in such an unpleasant manner." Turning to Hassan, Claude continued, "George was a copyist. We'll miss him."

Intrigued, Hassan raised his eyebrows. "Was he good?"

Claude appeared offended. "Of course, he was good. The Louvre only lets the most talented copyists work there."

"Have many people have died falling down stairs at the Louvre?" Ava asked, trying to get more information

Claude cleared his throat and stared at her coldly. "Since I've been there, George is the first one. We've had heart attacks. People have slipped on floors. They've run into statues. We've had countless sprained wrists and ankles. We even had a concussion or two. But people do not go to the Louvre to die... or to see dead bodies. I hope this is the last death we'll have. It's a stain on the reputation of a great institution."

"Is there going to be a memorial service?" Hassan asked.

Claude's expression changed, a wave of emotion ran across his face. "George was well-loved. There will be a memorial service tomorrow morning at the St. Roch Church."

"The church where famous artists have their memorial services?" Ava asked, trying to learn as much as possible.

Claude nodded. "The French playwright Molière is

buried there. George Starr is going out with the best of them. He is, indeed, a lucky man."

"If you have to die, you might as well die in Paris," Hassan said.

"That's true," Claude replied. "Paris is the place to die."

Ava doubted that most non-Parisians would agree with them. However, she kept her thoughts to herself.

"Now show me my paperweight," Claude said.

Hassan leaned over and pulled a package out of the carrier bag where he kept his special items. He unwrapped a paperweight and handed it to Claude.

Claude's eyes lit up. He turned it over in his hand and caressed it. "It's a *bijou*, a jewel. I can always count on you to find what I'm looking for."

Beaming, Hassan took it back and began to wrap it up again.

Claude turned to Ava. "*Mademoiselle*, a word of professional advice if I may. Sometimes, it's good to let sleeping dogs lie."

Ava was speechless. With those words, Claude Monet was letting her know that something was suspicious about George Starr's death!

"I'll call you know when I find the other items you're interested in," Hassan said as he put the wrapped paperweight in a bag.

Claude took it and glanced down the quay at Henri's stand. Seeing it was closed, he turned his attention back to Ava. He had a knowing look in his eye. "Please say hello to Henri for me. Tell him that I'm glad that Sext and DeAth is back together again."

CHAPTER 4

"I knew I could trust you the first moment I saw you. That's why I spoke to you," George Starr whispered as he looked up at Ava from the landing where he lay in a pool of blood.

"You're dead..." she murmured, stunned at George's miraculous resurrection.

"It takes more than falling down a flight of stairs to kill me," George replied with a wink.

"I'm so glad," Ava said. "I thought someone had murdered you."

Suddenly, a panicked look appeared in George's eyes. It was the same look of panic as in the café. "Ava! Watch out!"

Ava swirled around. Too late! A hand shoved her. She

stumbled backwards, missed the step and flew up in the air. "No!" she screamed as her body tumbled down the stone stairs, bouncing off each one.

When her body hit the last step, everything went black.

Choking with terror, Ava leapt up. Entangled in her bed covers, she fell out of bed and landed on her apartment's wooden floor.

The Louvre had vanished.

George Starr was gone.

And she was alive.

More shaken by her dream than she would like to admit, Ava stood up and tossed the covers on the bed. She sank to the floor as sunlight poured in through the glass skylight overhead. The entire apartment was aglow with light. It was going to be a beautiful day. She hoped it would be less eventful than yesterday.

Remembering her conversation with George in her dream, Ava was sad.

The George Starr she had met wouldn't be talking to anyone every again.

"I promise I'll catch your killer," Ava vowed under her breath as she checked the time.

It was 8 A.M.

She had two hours before George Starr's memorial

service. Yesterday afternoon, she had called the church several times to find out the time of the mass. No one had answered. She'd found the time on the church's website. The memorial service was scheduled for 10 A.M.

A strange sound caught her attention.

It was a loud high-pitched hiss.

It was coming from the kitchen.

Mercury!

Jumping up, Ava slipped her feet into bright bluebird blue Moroccan embroidered slippers and dashed across the open space apartment.

"I'm coming!" she shouted.

When she reached the kitchen, a black cat with green eyes was staring up at her with obvious discontent. Grumbling under her breath, Ava opened a kitchen cabinet, pulled out a box of dry cat food, poured it into a bowl and set it down in front of the cat.

Mercury circled the bowl, not entirely satisfied with its contents.

"Listen. You're lucky you're getting breakfast at all," Ava said as she crouched down next to him. "For all I know, you've already eaten breakfast ten times already!"

With a swing of his tail, Mercury ignored her and began to eat.

Ava had no idea what the cat's name really was. He was

well-groomed, well-fed and his coat was shiny. Ava called him Mercury because he appeared most mornings like the planet. He would slip in through the skylight overhead and wait for Ava to serve him breakfast. When she was slow to do so, he made his unhappiness known.

Ava put water on for tea and took some green *Genmaicha* tea out of a canister. This was no morning for coffee. She was on her way to a memorial service and needed to be calm.

She stared down at the cat and attempted to explain her strange state of mind to him.

"By speaking to me, George became more than a familiar stranger. He became an acquaintance, a possible friend… He might even have played a significant role in my life if he hadn't died so suddenly."

Mercury stopped eating and stared at her with his slanted green eyes.

"OK. Maybe we never would have spoken again if George had lived. But I'll never know that," Ava said dramatically.

Mercury went back to eating.

With a sigh, Ava poured hot water into the teapot and carried it over to the large wooden table. A bouquet of pink and red peonies was in a vase in the center of the table. The bouquet was from Benji.

Her cell phone rang. Ava dashed across the apartment,

grabbed the phone and checked the number.

It was Benji...

Sometimes, great minds did work together.

"Good morning, *cheri*," Ava said as she settled into a chair. "How are you?"

"Getting ready to go to bed. It's late in New York. First, I wanted to call and see how my little Ava was."

"Your little Ava is fine," Ava said, delighted to hear from him. Ava had met Benji a month earlier on the Yves Dubois's case that she and Henri had solved together. Benji was a doctoral student in medieval manuscripts. They had had a brief whirlwind romance. It wasn't a romance that made fireworks go off. It was what the French call "*une amitié amoureuse*", a romantic friendship. Whatever you called it, Benji had done wonders for her. Sadly, he had moved to New York to complete his doctorate. Their brief romance had comforted her. It had reassured her that she was not doomed to die an old maid.

"How is our little Mercury?" Benji asked.

Ava eyed the cat affectionately, not too affectionately, as Mercury did not really like people. That was fine with Ava as she wasn't especially fond of animals.

"He's eating his breakfast," she said.

"*C'est bon,*" Benji replied.

"It's Benji. He says hello," Ava said to the cat that

43

ignored her. Ava had been jealous of Mercury's relationship with Benji. For a cat that didn't like people, he had immediately taken to Benji. The two had bonded to the point where Mercury had completely ignored her. But now that Benji was gone, Mercury was grudgingly accepting Ava's presence once again. It was probably out of survival instinct. The day Mercury learned how to open the box of cat food; his relationship with Ava would be over.

"What's new?" Benji asked.

"Nothing," Ava replied.

There was a long silence on the other end.

"Benji, are you there?" Ava asked.

"When you say nothing, I get suspicious. That means something big, something incredibly important, something stupendously earth-shaking has happened... Am I right?"

"I witnessed a murder," Ava announced gravely.

On the other end of the line, Benji burst out laughing.

"It's not funny. One minute, George was speaking to Henri and me. A few seconds later, he was on the landing in the monumental double staircase in the Denon Wing of the Louvre, dead."

"George? George who? I don't remember you mentioning a George," Benji said with true alarm.

"George Starr. Henri and I had just met him, and then it was over," Ava acknowledged.

"You'd just met him, and he died?" Benji asked in disbelief. "Who killed him?"

"For now, it's an accident..." Ava responded as she poured tea into a porcelain teacup.

"What does Henri say?" Benji asked.

"That it's an accident. But when he has all the facts, he'll change his mind," Ava replied in a rushed tone.

There was silence on the other end.

Ava spoke before Benji could respond. "I have to get the facts. George spoke to me right before he died. We're cosmically linked. I have an obligation to unearth the truth. Besides, he's English. I owe it to him as a fellow Brit."

"What does Henri think of your poking around in this affair?" Benji asked, less than convinced by her explanation.

"Henri is French," Ava responded.

"What does that mean?" Benji asked. "And before you say something ridiculous, let me remind you that I'm French, too."

Ava let out a groan. "There's nothing wrong with you French. It's just that we English have a flair for this sort of thing. How many famous French detectives are there in literature?"

"Hercule Poirot?" Benji ventured.

"He's from Belgium," Ava replied.

"Maigret?"

"Yes, Maigret was French. But the author was from Belgium. Let's face it, France has great criminals. However, for detectives we Brits can't be beat."

There was a long silence on the other end of the phone.

"I meant that as a compliment," Ava said. "Great criminals are hard to find."

"Promise me you won't do anything dangerous," Benji said, now serious.

Ava hesitated. She didn't want to lie to him. After an eternity, she responded. "I promise!"

"And promise me that you will tell Henri before you do any sleuthing on your own. Don't forget the Canal St. Martin."

Ava sighed and fell silent. The Canal St. Martin was an inglorious episode where she had been pushed into the canal on her last case. Henri had been nearby and had rescued her.

"Ava???"

"I promise," Ava said.

"Good. Have a nice day, my *cherie.*"

"Sleep well, Benji," Ava said and hung up. She uncrossed her index and third finger on her left hand.

Mercury had stopped eating and was staring at her with disapproval.

"If I told Benji the truth he would only worry. Sometimes, life puts you in a situation where truth takes second place to your greater duty," Ava explained.

Ava strode across the apartment that had been cobbled together from a series of small rooms that were originally used for maids to a stairway in the corner. The stairs led to a small round room in a tower. She grabbed her laptop from the desk and brought it back down to the kitchen.

First things first.

It was time to see what the French press had written about George Starr's death.

As she sipped her tea, Ava typed George's name into a search engine. She frowned as she read the results.

Clearly, a death in the Louvre wasn't front page material at a time when the European Football Championship had just kicked off. There were a few small articles in the French press on the accident. Most writers used George's death to highlight other points.

One writer cited the statistics on the risk of dying in a museum. Ava was happy to read that it very low. Another story spoke about strange accidents that had killed people in French museums. In one such case, a smoker had stepped out into the museum courtyard for a cigarette during a storm and had been hit by lightning. Death was instantaneous.

One overly French centric article protested that for every dead foreign visitor -- hundreds, if not thousands, of French art works were at risk of being damaged or destroyed by the uncaring tourists.

Ava was astonished that there was nothing in the British press about George's accident. It was as if he didn't exist.

Yesterday evening, she had done some preliminary research on him. She had found a few references to George's participation in group shows in the South of France. But as there were no pictures of the artist, the articles might be speaking about a different George Starr.

Ava stood up and walked across the apartment. She stopped in front of her late Uncle Charles's record player and looked through his vintage collection of 60s rock albums. Prior to his days at New Scotland Yard, her uncle had been a roadie for famous groups. Over the years, he had assembled an incredible collection of albums from the period. Ava went through them looking for something to fit her mood. She stopped on an album by *The Velvet Underground.*

It was just what the doctor ordered.

As the first notes of "Sunday Morning" rang out through the apartment, Ava went to choose her outfit for the day.

It was time to get ready for George Starr's memorial service.

CHAPTER 5

The St. Roch Church was a 17th century late Baroque church on the busy rue Saint-Honoré in the 1st arrondissement of Paris. It was on the right bank of the Seine. The church was situated in the heart of the fashion district where top fashion brands touted their wares to fashionistas. This explained the extremely well-dressed people wandering past, looking as if they had stepped out of a photo shoot.

The St. Roch church was a block away from the *Comedié-Française*, the French national state theater that had its own troupe of actors. Maybe this was why famous French actors had their memorial services at the church. Coincidentally, the church was only five minutes from the Louvre where George Starr had met his untimely end.

Ava had promised herself that she would no longer use

the "*m*" word until she had some proof indicating that a murder had taken place. Until then, she was just out hunting for clues.

Today, her attire was part of her strategy.

To play the part, you had to look the part...

After much hesitation, she had chosen a simple black dress, simple but elegant. After all, this was Paris. She wore black strappy sandals and had pulled her long hair back under a black chiffon scarf. Due to the seriousness of the occasion, she had traded her signature red lipstick for a more understated pinkish beige shade that made her pale skin look even paler. She had topped this off with large black sunglasses that mourners always wore in films.

Ava crossed the busy street and strode up the stone steps toward the church. Its massive blue front doors were closed. A smaller door to the left of the blue doors was partly ajar. Skirting around tourists soaking up the rays on the church steps, Ava headed toward the smaller door. She slowed at the last minute and looked up at the sky.

It was going to be a beautiful day. It was a perfect day for a picnic or a stroll along the Seine. It was not a day to have a memorial service.

She tightened her black chiffon scarf under her chin, slipped through the side door and entered the church. The church was an enormous cavernous space with baroque arches, stained glass windows and simple wooden chairs. It was dark in the church. Her dark glasses made everything even darker. Reluctantly, she took them off and looked around to get her bearings.

A mass was underway.

The church was almost empty. People were scattered in chairs near the altar. Few were dressed in black. Many people looked like they had slipped into the cool church to escape the morning heat rather than attend a memorial service.

Maybe this wasn't George Starr's memorial service...

Ava swiveled her head around and noticed a tall bald man in his thirties, dressed in a casual navy blue suit. The man was watching the ceremony from the back of the church. He didn't appear especially distraught.

She crept over to him. "Is this George Starr's memorial service?"

The man stared at her. He raised a finger to his lips and nodded.

After mouthing a silent "thank you", Ava tiptoed up the side aisle and slid into a seat behind two mourners. She slipped her sunglasses back on.

She preferred to see and not be seen.

The first part was easier said than done as it took her a few minutes of squinting before her eyes adapted, and she was able to see around her.

The turnout for George Starr's service was less than overwhelming.

The small group of mourners was evenly distributed on both sides of the aisle. Ava estimated that there were about twenty people in total. Huge floral arrangements were on both sides of the altar. She wondered if they weren't left over from another service. She was relieved to see there was no casket.

Her uncle hadn't had a casket or a church service when he had died. He had been cremated. Some friends from New Scotland Yard had then flown down to Gibraltar to throw his ashes into the sea.

"Charlie always said he'd swim with the sharks one day," one of Charles's oldest friends had said with real affection at his memorial party.

Instead of a traditional memorial service, Henri had thrown a party for Charles's friends with good French wine, excellent food and Charles's favorite music. There was also whiskey, one of her uncle's favorite drinks. Charles had bought a case of expensive Scottish whiskey years before his death and had set it aside for the occasion. It was a gesture that everyone appreciated.

Looking around the dark church, Ava wondered if George Starr would have preferred a party to this rather bleak service.

The dramatic baritone voice coming from the altar caught Ava's attention.

A priest in a green and white robe was speaking from a wooden pulpit. As he spoke, he gripped it and leaned forward, his fingers tightened around the pulpit with each word. "George Starr was an artist, an artist whose trajectory can be compared to that of a shooting star... short and brilliant."

A striking woman in her thirties with angel-like blond hair that cascaded down her back was in the front row on the opposite side of the aisle. She was weeping. Apart from Ava, she was the only person dressed in black.

The priest continued his speech. He looked left and right as he spoke as if addressing each person, individually. "For those of us who knew George and loved him, he was unique and special." The priest paused. When he spoke again, his voice was tender, almost tearful. "George was our brother. He was a friend to all. And now, he's watching over all of us from above... We will miss you, George." The priest raised his hands in the air and looked up. "You are with our heavenly father."

A dark-haired man in a white shirt sitting in the front row next to the blond-haired woman began to applaud. A few disapproving stares and loud whispers put an end to that.

"George would be horrified by this travesty. He never

went to church in his life," a woman with short black hair cut in a 1920's bob said to the thin ethereal woman with long red hair who was seated next to her.

Both women were directly in front of Ava. All she had to do to eavesdrop was lean forward.

The red-haired woman shrugged her head in a gesture toward the weeping woman in the first row. "This is a typical Laura move. George wasn't even cold in the ground, and she's already rewriting history."

The woman with the dark bob shook her head. "Marina, what does it matter? George is gone, and he's not coming back." She began to weep.

Marina, the red-haired woman, reached out and squeezed the other woman's hand. "It'll be OK. I promise…"

The priest was now at the altar, finishing the mass. When the first notes of organ music began to play, he opened his hands and looked out at the mourners in the church. He looked up and raised his hands to heaven. "Amen."

"Amen," everyone chimed in together.

The priest left the altar as the organ music echoed loudly through the church. People stood up and left. Some stopped to speak with others. Other people exited as quickly as possible.

Ava waited until the two women in front of her had left before getting up. She was the last one to leave the church.

When she stepped outside, two small groups of people were speaking at the top of the steps. The first group consisted of the blond-haired woman, the man in the white shirt who had clapped and the bald man Ava had spoken with. The second group was made up of the two women who had been seated in front of Ava during the service.

Ava eyed each group. If she were to learn anything, she would have to make a move. She decided to begin with the two women.

Nothing ventured, nothing gained, she told herself.

Before she could move toward them, Marina, the red-haired woman, strode up to Ava. The woman with a bob followed her.

"George's death was a tragedy," Marina said. "Are you a friend of his?"

"An acquaintance," Ava replied cautiously. "I was devastated to learn about his death."

The woman with the short bob wiped a tear from her eye. "We were all devastated."

"I'm Ava Sext," Ava said suddenly.

The woman with the bob frowned. "You're English?"

"Yes. From London."

Marina's expression clouded over. "Have you been in Paris long?"

"A while. I'm staying at my uncle's place," Ava said.

Marina took in the information with a frown.

The woman with the bob stared at Ava, uneasy. "I'm Apple Fenon." Anticipating Ava's reaction, she added, "My father was an archeology buff. He named me Aphrodite. I chose Apple early on." As she spoke, Apple's strong features melded together into a singular beauty that was striking.

"Marina Vasiliev," the red-haired woman said, introducing herself.

The woman spoke with an accent that Ava guessed was Russian.

Marina looked younger than Apple. Ava guessed that she was probably in her early thirties, while Apple was in her forties.

"How do you know George?" Marina asked Ava.

Ava stuck to the truth. She wasn't a good liar. She had decided it was easier to tell the truth – just not the whole truth. "I met George at the Louvre. In the Café Mollien. We were chatting about the weather. I'm afraid that's something with English do wherever we meet. He recommended that I take a drawing class."

Apple smiled tenderly. Tears came into her eyes. Marina eyed her with concern.

From Apple's reaction, Ava knew she had hit a bulls-eye.

"George believes that art is for anyone. Sorry, believed," Apple said, holding back a sob.

"Are you artists?" Ava asked.

Marina remained silent. Ava sensed she was being judged.

Wiping a tear from her eye, Apple answered for both of them. "Marina works in art restoration. I'm an artist."

"Apple could be a great painter if she wanted. I wish I could paint like her," Marina said.

"George told me he was a copyist," Ava added, fishing for information.

Apple shook her head. "George was more than a copyist. He was a magician. He could see a painting and recreate it. If asked to choose the better painting, I'm sure most artists would have chosen George's version over their own."

Thinking back to George's half-finished painting, Ava nodded. "That is a gift..."

"Not if you're an artist," Marina responded. "Artists need to create their own work." She paused and stared at Ava. "I hold a small drawing class in the Louvre. There are only a five of us. You're welcome to come. It's every Thursday."

"I'd love to," Ava replied quickly. "George's death was a warning to me."

Apple paled and raised her hand to her throat. "A warning. What do you mean?"

"If I want to learn to draw, I should do it now. You never know when time will run out," Ava replied.

Apple broke into tears. Ava could have kicked herself for her insensitive remark.

Trying to save the situation, Ava continued, "Tomorrow's Thursday. Is there a class?"

Marina nodded. "Life goes on. 9:15 under the pyramid. We meet at the bottom of the escalator to the Denon Wing."

Apple raised her eyebrows. "The Denon Wing? Do you think that's wise?"

"We started drawing a painting in the Grand Gallery of the Denon Wing last week. I don't see why we should stop just because George died there," Marina replied.

Apple appeared conflicted. "Are you sure you want to hold class tomorrow?"

"George is dead. We're alive. If the situation were reversed, what would George do?" Marina said with a knowing glance.

Apple sighed. "We both know the answer to that. George would insist that art was life."

"What do I need to bring?" Ava asked.

"A sketchbook, some pencils and an eraser," Marina responded.

Just then, a loud argument broke out in the other group. Looking up, Marina and Apple froze.

The tall bald-headed man from the back of the church shoved the dark-haired man in the white shirt. "Marc, you're not dealing with George now. You're dealing with me. So watch it."

The dark-haired man, Marc, appeared inebriated. He was not in the least bit intimidated by the bald-headed man's words. In a show of bravado, he pushed him back. "Don't touch me, Enzo! You'll regret it if you do."

Laura, the blond-haired woman who had been weeping during the service, grabbed Marc by the arm. "That's enough, Marc. Don't you have enough problems?"

Her words caused him to reel back. Shaken, he turned and staggered drunkenly down the steps.

Laura and Enzo watched him. Laura took Enzo's arm. Enzo glanced at Apple and Marina. He eyed the departing Marc.

"I'd better go help him before he gets hit by a car," Enzo said in a loud voice as he hurried down the steps.

With an unreadable expression on her face, Laura watched him walk off. Immediately, she turned and joined Ava, Marina and Apple.

"Marc is drinking too much. He lacks discipline," she said to Apple and Marina. With a warm smile, she spoke to Ava. "I don't believe we've met. I'm Laura Gossal."

Ava smiled. "Ava Sext."

"Did you come from London?" Laura asked.

Sensing that there was more to this question than met

the eye, Ava hedged her response. "Originally. But I've been staying at my uncle's flat in Paris for a while."

"How lovely," Laura responded, no longer interested. Hearing loud voices, she turned. Without a word, she hurried down the steps to Marc and Enzo who were now arguing.

"What was that about?" Apple asked Marina.

Marina eyed Laura and the two men. Ignoring Apple's question, she turned to Ava. "You'll have to excuse us. The shock of losing someone affects people differently. Don't forget, 9:15 tomorrow if you're still interested."

"I'll be there," Ava said.

"Give me your phone number in case class is cancelled," Marina said.

Ava hesitated. She didn't want to give Marina her cell number. She took a small notebook out of her bag, ripped a page out and wrote her Uncle Charles's home number on it. As she handed the paper to Marina, another paper fell out of her notebook and flew up through the air. Enzo caught it at the bottom of the steps. He eyed it and walked up to the women. He handed the paper back to Ava.

"You almost lost your concert ticket. I'm Enzo Berrardi."

"Ava Sext."

Before Ava could say more, Marc started shouting at Laura.

Enzo eyed him and sighed. "Duty calls." He hurried back toward Laura and Marc.

Marina folded the paper with Ava's number on it and put it in her pocket. "Don't forget, 9:15!"

"I'll be there," Ava said.

Sensing the discussion was over, Ava went down the steps slowly. Pulling her scarf tighter, she crossed the rue Saint-Honoré to the other side and headed toward the Tuileries Garden. As she walked, she could feel eyes on her.

You're a hit, Ava… Everyone is curious about you.

Somehow, Ava sensed that wasn't what she wanted when a murderer was on the loose.

CHAPTER 6

The moment Ava crossed the busy rue de Rivoli and entered the Tuileries Garden, she removed her black chiffon scarf and shook her long dark hair free. She took her red lipstick out of her pocket and swiped it on over the beige lipstick. Instantly, she felt better.

As the French say, *"c'est les petites choses"*... It's the little things that make you happy.

Skirting past the goats that were happily eating the grass in the garden, Ava headed directly to the Arc de Triomphe, the same arch she had been looking at yesterday when George Starr had appeared in her life.

Poor George!

Thinking about him set her mind to work. There wasn't a second to waste if she wanted to solve his murder. As she wound her way through the crowds of tourists and touts selling miniature Eiffel Towers in every color of the rainbow, she ran over what she had learned during George's memorial service.

One... There was tension in George's group of friends, and the explosive Marc had problems.

Two... There was something "off" about the glamorous Laura who had confronted her. Why had she wanted to know if Ava had come from London?

Three... Apple had been alarmed when Ava had spoken of a warning, while Marina had taken the comment a whole different way.

Four... There was the elephant in the room. Or in this case, the missing elephant... Where was the woman who had screamed and vanished in the Louvre? There must be a reason for her absence at church today.

As Ava's mind turned to the screaming woman, she couldn't shake the feeling that there was something familiar about her. She couldn't put her finger on what that was.

Ava was excited about the drawing class. It would give her a chance to speak with Marina and learn more about George. However, Ava would need to keep her wits about her. The murderer would not like it if he learned that she was investigating George's death.

She also had to find a way to meet the other people she

had spoken with after the memorial service. Someone must have an inkling about the reasons for George's death. The murderer might even be one of them!

When she reached the Arc de Triomphe in the Carrousel Garden at the entrance to the Tuileries Garden, Ava halted. She stood under the enormous arch. She gazed up at the window in the Louvre where she had been sitting yesterday.

Life was so fleeting.

One moment, you're in the Café Mollien having a cappuccino and an apple tart, and the next moment you're dead.

George had died yesterday.

Tomorrow, it might be her.

Ava calmed her imagination. She should be looking for a murderer, not contemplating her own earthly demise.

Suddenly, a pigeon flew toward her and landed at her feet, flapping its wings and cooing loudly. Startled, Ava stepped back and bumped into a woman taking a selfie.

"Excuse me," Ava said.

Instead of hearing her own voice, Ava heard George Starr's voice apologizing to her after he had tripped and almost fallen onto the table.

In the aftermath of his death, Ava had completely forgotten about that fall. In a flash, she understood its significance.

It might even hold the answer to the case.

She began to run. Pigeons flew up and scattered in her wake.

As Ava crossed the Pont du Carrousel, the car bridge that linked the Seine's right and left banks in front of the Louvre, she felt faint. Her mouth was so dry that she could barely swallow.

She had made a terrible mistake.

One of the most important rules in sleuthing was to pay attention to what was happening around you. After George's death, she had let her imagination run wild and had missed an essential element. She hoped that it wasn't too late to rectify this error.

When she reached the left bank, she slowed. She hadn't told Henri that she was going to the service. Now she would appear at her stand looking like a widow from a 1950's Italian film. For a brief instant, she considered going home to change.

It was too late for that.

She needed to find the cloth bag with her art materials and see what George had slipped in it.

That's what she should have noticed immediately...

When he had walked up to their table, George had been holding a small sketchbook in his hand. When he ran off, the sketchbook was gone.

That could only mean one thing... George had left it at the table.

The only place he could have left it was in Ava's bag, which had been hanging on the chair next to her. Ava remembered his falling over. At the time, she thought it was strange. Now, she realized it was deliberate.

Another thought popped into her mind.

Henri knew that George Starr had left his sketchbook in her bag. Being the careful observer that he was, Henri would have noticed that the man had a sketchbook when he arrived and didn't have one when he left. After all, he had had noticed the titanium dioxide paint on George's hand.

Could the sketchbook have fallen on the ground?

Ava closed her eyes and pulled an image of the floor from the depths of her memory.

Nothing had been on it.

Another thought occurred to her, a more disquieting thought: Her bag had been left unattended when she and Henri were at the railing after George's fall.

Anyone could have taken the sketchbook... including the murderer.

Feeling horrible, Ava lurched toward her stand. She slowed when she passed by Hassan who was leaning against the stone wall.

Eyeing her outfit, he raised his eyebrows. "What's the occasion? A fancy dress party?"

"Can't a girl get dressed up?" Ava asked.

"What would be your reaction if I appeared at my stand tomorrow wearing a three-piece suit?" Hassan asked.

"I decided to dress up and take a walk. I'm not a slave to my stand," Ava replied, well-aware she wasn't fooling him.

"Suit yourself. But Claude told me he saw you at George's service," Hassan said.

Ava went numb. "Claude? Claude Monet? Your friend who heads security at the Louvre?"

Hassan nodded. "My friend who heads security at the Louvre."

Ava knitted her eyebrows. "I didn't see him there."

"That's why Claude works in security. You only see him when he wants you to," a familiar voice said.

Henri!

Felling guilty, Ava turned to him. "I had to go to the service to discover what was going on."

"And that is?" Patient, Henri waited for her explanation.

Before she could speak, Ava noticed that Henri was dressed in a dark suit. Henri never wore a suit. There could only be one reason he was wearing a dark suit on a warm June day, and that wasn't possible...

Unless it was.

"I didn't see you at the service," Ava said with a frown. "Where were you?"

"Claude and I got there early. We were at a side altar. No one noticed us," Henri answered. "The ceremony was very touching. The priest gave a wonderful speech. One thing puzzled Claude though..." Henri said, his voice trailing off.

"What? What was it?" Ava asked, sure that she was about to learn something important.

"He wondered how you could see with your dark sunglasses on!" Henri said.

Hassan burst out laughing.

Ava pushed her sunglasses up on her head and pulled her shoulders back. "I have important things to do." She walked off to her stand that Hassan had opened. Her heart beating, she prayed that the bag with the sketchbooks was still there. When she reached her stand, she looked in the space on the left where she kept her belongings.

The bag wasn't there.

Spinning around, she eyed her lawn chair that was under the tree. Her straw hat was on it as was the book she had been trying to read for days. Her thermos was on the ground.

But the cloth bag was nowhere in sight.

Someone had taken it.

Barely able to breathe, Ava hurried over to Hassan who was now speaking with a customer.

"Hassan," she said.

"Can it wait, Ava?" Hassan asked as he looked up from his discussion.

"No. It can't," Ava said.

Hassan nodded. "Go ahead."

"Did you see a cotton bag when you opened the stand this morning?"

Hassan rubbed his nose. "Yes. I hung it from your chair. I looked in it first. There was nothing worth stealing... only a couple of sketchbooks."

In shock, Ava walked back to her stand. She could feel her legs giving way beneath her. George Starr had entrusted her with an important clue to his death, and she had let it get away.

Ava scoured the ground around the chair. She sank into it as tears filled her eyes.

Henri strode over and looked down at her with pity. "I saw the bag hanging from your chair and thought it prudent to remove it."

"You have it?" Ava asked.

Henri nodded.

Ava took a deep breath. The dark clouds lifted. The bottomless abyss she had been plunging into vanished. George's clue was safe!

Henri handed the bag to her.

Ava took it and clutched it to her chest. *It was still possible to find George's murderer. It wasn't too late.*

When Ava looked inside the bag, Henri shook his head. "Not here."

Ava glanced behind them at the closed café. "Where do you want to go?"

"I'm house-sitting Mathilde's houseboat. We can go there," Henri said.

Mathilde Bompard was an investigating judge. She had been a judge for thirty years, although she didn't look a day over forty. Mathilde was a beautiful intelligent woman who was full of wit and charm. Ava suspected that Mathilde and Henri were closer than they would ever admit. If so, Ava would be delighted. Mathilde was a wonderful person.

Still clutching the bag, Ava rose to her feet. "Let's go!"

"We have to wait twenty minutes," Henri replied.

"Twenty minutes!" Ava exclaimed, puzzled. "What could be more important than the contents of the bag?"

Henri smiled. "As Café Zola is closed, I ordered lunch for us from a delivery "app". It will be here in twenty minutes."

Ava checked her impatience. Twenty minutes was nothing in the grand scheme of things. After all, it had taken her more than twenty-four hours to realize that she had the sketchbook. "Twenty minutes will be fine."

When Henri turned to return to his stand, Ava reached up and touched his arm.

"Thank you."

"We're partners in crime. We need to look out for each other."

Ava sank back into her lawn chair, clutching the bag. Her Uncle Charles might be dead, but he had left her Henri, and that was wonderful.

CHAPTER 7

As the houseboat rocked up and down on the Seine, Ava
hovered at the edge of the quay with her shoes in one hand.
Uneasy, she eyed the river's dark water. "Shouldn't you put
the boarding ramp down?"

"Just jump, Ava," Henri replied from the deck. He
grabbed the rope that moored the houseboat to the quay and
pulled the boat in as close as possible. "What's the worst that
can happen? You'll fall in the river and get wet," Henri said in
a vain attempt to be encouraging.

Looking down at the narrow space between the quay and
the boat and at the water splashing up next to her, Ava closed
her eyes and leapt into the air. When her feet hit the deck, she
opened her eyes. She was standing next to Henri in one piece,

totally dry.

"What happened to my fearless partner in sleuthing?" Henri teased.

Ava didn't answer.

Being fearless on a case was one thing. Being fearless on a daily basis was something entirely different.

Ava glanced down at the bag slung across her chest and removed it. She glanced inside it. The two sketchbooks were still there. Looking at their metal spirals, she took a deep breath.

Maybe, just maybe, she was holding the answer to George's death.

Henri had more important matters on his mind than investigating the contents of the bag. For Henri, it was lunchtime and that meant lunch.

He picked up the bag that the food deliveryman had delivered minutes earlier and strode to the middle of the deck. Although you would have a hard time finding the deck through the riot of flowers, bushes and trees that Mathilde had planted everywhere.

Mathilde's houseboat was a floating botanical garden. There were flowering plants, climbing rose bushes and large terra cotta pots filled with aromatic herbs.

In the early afternoon heat, Ava could smell the heavy odor of rosemary, thyme and lavender perfuming the air. It reminded her of long lazy summer vacations in the south of France with her late uncle, afternoons where they did nothing but eat and read.

"How long is Mathilde gone for?" Ava asked as she sank down onto one of the comfortable cushions scattered on a Tunisian kilim rug.

"Just a week. She's off to South Africa to give a speech at a law conference," Henri replied as he spread an embroidered tablecloth on a low table. He opened the large market umbrella to shade their lunch.

"Are you staying here all week?" Ava asked, curious as to how long Henri could be lured away from his house. Henry had a small house in the center of Paris near the Paris Observatory. The house had a large garden where Henri grew vegetables. Room after room was filled with books, papers and art objects. The chaos was done in such an artistic manner that Henri's house could have featured in any of the upscale decorating magazines that the French adored. That Henri accepted to be lured from his lair, so to speak, showed the strength of his friendship with the houseboat's owner.

"Yes, I'll be here all week. Mathilde prefers to have someone stay here during the summer when she's away. It's to prevent tourists from camping out on the deck."

"What about your garden?" Ava asked. The month of June was crucial to the heirloom vegetables that Henri grew.

"Hassan has moved in while I'm gone."

Ava raised her eyebrows, surprised.

"Don't worry. He has a green thumb. Come August,
you'll have tomatoes."

Henri disappeared inside the boat. Minutes later, he
came out with a several smaller cushions. He threw them on
top of the bigger ones. Ava positioned two small cushions
behind her back and moved the cloth bag next to her. She
was dying to see what was in it but resisted the urge.

They were dealing with murder.

Any investigation needed to be properly done.

Henri opened a bottle of red wine and sniffed the cork.
He nodded, smiling. "It's from a friend's vineyard in
Provence. A simple red for a warm day." Henri poured Ava
and himself a glass.

Ava sipped the wine. It was divine. "If this is your idea
of a simple red, what do you consider a great wine?"

Henri sank down onto a cushion in the shade of the
market umbrella and unpacked lunch. It was from a famous
Greek caterer. There were lots of little plastic containers.
Ava's heart soared as Henri opened each one and spread
them out across the table, announcing the contents as if they
were beauty pageant contestants.

"Kalamata olives, smoked salmon and blinis, eggplant
caviar, hummus, tabbouleh salad, octopus salad and

marinated artichoke hearts. There's also an assortment of Greek pastries for dessert," Henri said as he struggled to fit the feast on the table. Eyeing the final spread, Henri nodded. "This should do."

Unable to resist, Ava popped a Kalamata olive into her mouth. It was delicious.

Solemn, Henri lifted his wine glass in the air. "To George!"

With a lump in her throat, Ava raised her glass. "To George!"

She and George had only met once, but they were fellow travelers in a foreign land and thus linked by geography. Since she was present at his death, their destinies had also become entwined.

"Did you look inside?" Henri asked, eying the cloth bag.

Ava shook her head as she filled up a plate with food from each of the containers. "I prefer that we look at it together. If I'd opened it myself, my mind would have raced off. I would have come up with a million half-baked theories."

"There's still time for that," Henri said with a warm smile.

She ignored his teasing. "If we open it together, we can analyze what we find, calmly and methodically." A doubt entered her mind. "You didn't look at it, did you?"

Henri threw his head back, feigning indignation. "Ava!"

She smiled. "Sorry." Another thought came to her. "You saw George put it in my bag." It wasn't a question, it was an affirmation.

"I did," Henri confessed.

"Why didn't you say anything?" Ava asked as she squeezed lemon onto her salmon.

"I wasn't sure if anyone else had seen George do it. Given the circumstances of his death, I didn't want to draw any more attention to the bag than necessary."

Remembering that she had left it at the table while they were at the railing, Ava paled.

Before she could speak, Henri shook his head. "My eyes never left the bag the entire time. No one touched it."

Ava smiled.

Henri took a sip of wine and sampled the octopus salad. "I suggest we start with what we've each learned."

"Each?" Ava asked, raising her eyebrows.

Henri sat back. "Claude Monet went to the memorial service for a reason this morning. The head of security at the Louvre just doesn't take a morning off the day after an incident like George's death."

"So he suspects something's wrong? Did he say what?" Ava asked, excited.

"For the record, it was an accident. George Starr was

77

running down the stairs. He bumped into someone, lost his balance and fell. The security cameras captured his run down the stairs and didn't see anything unusual. For the police and the Louvre, the case is closed. That doesn't mean that Claude doesn't want to find out more. Call it professional curiosity... Claude used to be with the DSGE."

The DSGE, the *General Directorate for External Security* belonged to the French Ministry of Defense. It was an intelligence service tasked with keeping France's interests abroad safe. If Claude Monet had worked for the DSGE that meant he was the ultimate professional. But that didn't tell Ava what she needed to know.

"Did the cameras film what happened in the café?" Ava asked.

"Unfortunately, they were aimed at the door to the outside terrace and at the cash register. They didn't capture anything that happened in the café."

"Who is George Starr?" Ava asked. "There's more to this than meets the eye. When I looked him up on the web, there was almost nothing about him."

Henri took another sip of wine. "It's a long story. George Starr was born George Alistair Montague the 6th."

"An aristocrat?"

Henri nodded. "His family goes back to the twelfth century. Unfortunately, his grandfather gambled away all the family money and had to sell the family home and land. George's father became a barrister and married well."

"And George?" Ava asked. George didn't seem like the barrister type.

"He went to the Royal College of Art in London."

The Royal College of Art was a prestigious institution. Artists like Tracey Emin, David Hockney and Peter Blake had gone there.

Puzzled, Ava frowned. "How did George Alistair Montague the 6th become George Starr?"

"He had an unfortunate run-in with the law. He robbed a country house. He was caught. The owner, his cousin, forgave him. But the police still charged George with fencing stolen goods. His father disowned him. George moved to France and became George Starr."

"Has he been in France long?"

Henri poured wine into each of their glasses.

"Twenty years or so. He lived in the south of France for a long time. He spent a year or two in Brussels and Amsterdam. He's been in Paris for eighteen months."

"That's not long," Ava said. "Was that really his painting we saw at the Louvre?"

"Yes. Claude said that some of the curators thought he was a genius but…" Henri paused and took a sip of wine.

"But?" Ava said, anxious for Henri to get to the point.

"George was a hothead. When people offered to buy his paintings, he'd refuse. He even ripped one in half with a knife in front of a Louvre curator, claiming that the only thing that mattered was the moment an artist made a work. Only then was the artist working with life. Once the painting was painted, it was dead. In order for it to live again, someone had to awaken it."

"How did they do that?" Ava asked, perplexed.

"By copying it. Don't forget that the ancient Egyptians believed that a copy was imbued with the same power as the original. That's why they buried small replicas of objects with the dead."

Ava frowned. "Why did George choose us?"

"We were the wrong people in the right spot," Henri replied. "Until the school group arrived, the café was almost empty. If someone was following him, we were the only people there. When he heard your accent, it was providence."

"He wasn't worried when he first came to speak with us," Ava said. "In fact, he seemed almost disappointed when he spoke with me."

Henri frowned. "I hadn't noticed that. But you're right. He did seem disappointed."

Content that she had scored a point, Ava continued, "If George hadn't died. I would still have his sketchbook."

"If he'd lived, I trust he would have found you. You're

the only Ava Sext in Paris. If George slipped the sketchbook in your bag that meant he didn't have a choice."

"No, he didn't," Ava said, remembering the panic in George's eyes. Somehow, all this thinking had given her an appetite. She helped herself to more salmon.

Henri leaned back against the cushions. "What did you learn at church? By the way, your outfit was more grieving widow than sad friend. I hope that doesn't cause you problems."

"That would add an interesting twist to the tale," Ava said. "I learned that George has a group of friends. For some reason, they're not on the friendliest of terms. The man who applauded in church, Marc, was drunk. According to Laura Gossal, the blond-haired weeping woman, he has problems."

"What type of problems?"

"I don't know. But when Laura made a remark about them, Marc went white and stumbled away. Before that, he got in an argument with the bald-headed man, Enzo Berrardi. Laura pulled them apart. She's tougher than she looks."

"Is she an artist?" Henri asked, trying to get a take on who was who.

"I don't know. The two women in front of me both work in art. The woman with the black bob is Aphrodite Fenon, known as Apple. She's French and an artist. Marina Vasiliev, the redhead, is Russian and works in art restoration.

Laura organized the service. Apple and Marina said that George would have been horrified by a church service." Ava looked at Henri, puzzled. "How did Laura manage to book such a famous church for an unknown artist?"

"George helped restore the paintings in the church. He even painted copies of two paintings that went missing during the French revolution using period texts and descriptions from tax records to recreate them. George was well-loved by the pastor."

"Did Claude know anyone at the service?" Ava asked.

Henri nodded. "Your two women… Apple and Marina are often in the Louvre. Apple is also a copyist. Marina brings small groups to the Louvre for drawing."

"And Laura? The blond-haired weeping woman?"

"She works in a gallery. Claude has seen her with George in the Louvre in the past, but he doesn't know more than that."

Ava frowned. "The woman who screamed wasn't at the church this morning. Does Claude know who she is?"

"Claude promised to see if he could find her in the security tapes. With all the chaos that George's death caused, one scream, more or less, didn't register on anyone's radar."

"I only saw the woman her for a second, but there was something so familiar about her."

"Unfortunately, I only saw her from behind," Henri said

as poured himself another glass of wine. When he went to pour some in Ava's glass, she hesitated and accepted.

When in France...

She took a sip and then pulled the cloth bag in front of her. "Ready?"

"I was wondering when you'd get to it," Henri said.

"There's a time for everything," Ava responded calmly.

Henri cleared off the table, putting the dishes and containers on a tray. He wiped the table clean.

"Now we'll learn what George wanted to hide so desperately," Ava said as she removed the contents from the bag. The first thing she took out was the notebook that Hassan had bought her at Sennelier, the famous art store on the Quai Voltaire that was located near their stands. Then she took out a clear plastic pencil case with different pencils, an eraser and a pencil sharpener in it. A tube of Ava's favorite red lipstick was also in the case. The last item she took out was a small sketchpad.

George's sketchbook.

Ava opened it carefully. Its pages were blackened with tiny drawings. Some were drawings of torsos or arms. Others were of faces. Still other pages had landscapes drawn on them. And oddly, there were pages and pages of hares and hunters. Nothing was written anywhere in the sketchbook.

"It's full of very classical drawings," Ava said, puzzled.

"Why would he want to hide this?

Henri took the sketchbook from her and flipped through its pages slowly. "The drawings meant something. Otherwise, George wouldn't have hidden them and run off. This sketchbook was important enough that he died for it."

"How are we going to find out what it means?" Ava asked, disappointed that it didn't contain a smoking gun that would tell them who the murderer was.

"I'm not an art expert. I'll take a photo of some of the pages and send them to Ali," Henri said. "He'll be able to find out for us."

"He's in Switzerland at an art fair…" Ava protested.

"He has his cell phone with him," Henri responded. "Today, distance is no obstacle." He took out his cell phone, snapped a few photos and sent them off to Ali with a short text asking him to be discrete.

When Henri had finished, Ava took the sketchbook from him and paged through it again, this time more slowly. "The drawings are wonderful. They're so full of life. But I still don't see why someone would kill for them."

"That's what we need to discover," Henri said.

Suddenly, his every sense was alert. He eyed the quay that was packed with strolling people, enjoying the sunny afternoon.

Alarmed, Ava studied the quay. "Do you think someone

followed us here?"

"If George Starr was killed for these drawings, we have to be careful. What's your next step?" Henri asked.

"I have a drawing class tomorrow morning at the Louvre. Marina is giving it," Ava responded.

Henri frowned. "You might be putting yourself in danger."

"I have to go. I owe it to George."

Henri sighed. "You're pigheaded, just like your uncle. Be careful. Don't be surprised if you see me nearby."

"What are you going to do?" Ava asked.

"Follow the money," Henri said.

Ava frowned.

"George refused to sell his paintings. He doesn't have family money. I need to discover what he was living off of. His clothing didn't look like the clothing of a starving artist."

Ava went to put George's sketchbook in her bag.

Henri shook his head. "It will be safer with me."

Ava didn't protest. Henri was right.

CHAPTER 8

Worried that she was late, Ava dashed across the Pont des Arts Bridge toward the Louvre. She zigzagged around the artists that were setting up their easels on the pedestrian bridge. Her own failed attempts at drawing the evening before made her appreciate their work even more. As she slowed to study a painting of the Eiffel Tower, she realized that it wasn't easy to draw or paint something and have it look like what you were drawing or painting. If she drew the Eiffel Tower, she feared it would look like a clothespin with legs.

Yesterday evening, she had stayed up drawing to get ready for her class today. Hours of vain attempts to draw the vase of flowers on the kitchen table had taught her that you needed to coordinate your hand and mind... teach the two to tango, so to speak.

Ava sighed.

If the drawings in her bag were a reflection of that principle, it showed that she had two left feet.

Exhausted from her artistic efforts, she had fallen into a deep sleep. She would still be under the covers, dreaming about painting the ceiling of the Sistine Chapel with Michelangelo, if Mercury hadn't appeared at the edge of her bed, mewing loudly for his breakfast.

Worried that she would be late, she had fed Mercury and gotten dressed. Now, she was in desperate need of a coffee. Seeing the glass pyramid that housed the museum's entrance before her, she checked the time.

She had a good half hour before she was to meet Marina. That left her plenty of time for a strong coffee and a crispy croissant.

Ava waltzed through the priority line at the Louvre, flashing her journalist card, a relic from her social media days and took the escalator down into the atrium.

If there ever was a modern Tower of Babel, it was the atrium under the Louvre's glass pyramid. Speaking every language under the sun, a sea of tourists trooped across it to reach the subterranean passageways that would lead them to the various wings that held the museum's treasures.

Ava held back a desire to flee. She didn't like crowds. In fact, she hated them. But forty-eight hours earlier, fate had led her to the Denon Wing of the Louvre and George Starr. Now, duty had brought her back.

She took the escalator up to the mezzanine and bought a coffee and a croissant from a stand. She sat at a table that overlooked the escalator to the Denon Wing where she was to meet Marina and the group.

Ava didn't want to appear too early or too late.

Too early would make her look overeager and that might appear unseemly in light of George's recent death. Too late and the group might leave without her.

Sipping the murky brown liquid in her cup, Ava pulled out her sketchpad and looked at the drawings she had worked on the night before. Eyeing the result, she sighed. The best anyone could say was that she was a beginner, a true beginner, and that was a generous appraisal of her talent.

Whoever had created the drawings in George's sketchbook had real talent. In the drawings, the arms looked liked they could reach out and grip you. You could almost see the blood pulsing through the hunters' veins.

Ava sighed. George hadn't been killed because of the beauty or skill of the drawings. He had been killed because the drawings meant something. She and Henri needed to discover what that was.

She checked her phone. There was no news from Henri or Ali. Ali had texted them back yesterday to say that he was looking into the sketchbook.

Ava glanced around to see if Henri was nearby. There was no sign of him or Claude Monet, not that Claude knew she was coming to the Louvre this morning. However, Ava had a feeling that Claude, like Henri, would appear when you least expected him to appear. She found that comforting.

Ava closed her sketchbook and eyed her surroundings.

Overhead, bright sunlight was pouring through the glass pyramid casting intricate patterns of light on the atrium's floor below. The patterns appeared and disappeared as people passed over them. Most people didn't even notice the light or how beautiful it was.

Ava couldn't claim to be more aware of her surroundings than they were. Two days ago, George Starr had slipped a sketchbook in her bag, and she hadn't noticed it.

That was a major failure for a sleuth -- even a new-to-the-field sleuth.

With firm resolve, Ava vowed to pay attention to what was going on around her or at least try. Seeing a small group of people gather at the bottom of the escalator to the Denon Wing, she gulped down the last sip of bitter liquid that pretended to be coffee, crushed her paper cup, took one last bite out of the cardboard-like croissant and tossed everything into a trashcan. She took the escalator down.

When she reached the group, they walked off behind a guide who was issuing instructions in German, leaving Ava alone at the bottom of the escalator.

Frowning, she scanned the area for a familiar face.

Marina was nowhere in sight.

It was 9:25. Surely, some members of the drawing group should have appeared by now.

Maybe the class had been cancelled...

"I'm not the only one who likes to be early," a lilting woman's voice said.

Startled, Ava turned. She smiled as she recognized Apple walking toward her.

Apple was dressed in a blue skirt and a simple blue sleeveless top. Her dark bob was pushed behind her ears and she wasn't wearing any makeup. Her look was very artsy. After Henri's remarks on the Italian widow outfit that she had worn to George's memorial service, Ava had gone back to her tried and true uniform of jeans, black sandals and a white t-shirt. To add a dash of color, she had thrown on a vintage pink and green flowered silk scarf she had bought at a Paris flea market. As she had been in a hurry that morning, her dark hair was pulled back in a ponytail.

Apple was tense when she reached Ava.

"Where are the others?" Ava asked, looking around.

"The class was cancelled. As Marina couldn't find the paper with your number on it, she asked me to come and tell you," Apple said.

Ava had the clear impression that something was bothering Apple, something more than George's death.

Apple pointed to a bag hanging over her shoulder. "I'm going to sketch today. If you want, you can come with me."

"Thank you. I'd love to," Ava said with true enthusiasm. This was her chance to get information about George's death. She intended to learn all she could.

Ava followed Apple up the escalator. Watching the woman from behind, Ava was more and more convinced that something had happened that Apple wasn't telling her. It was Ava's sleuthing sixth sense at work.

As they waited in line to enter the Denon Wing, Ava spoke, "George said that being a copyist was a privilege."

Hearing George's name, Apple smiled sadly. "He was right. It is a privilege. We were some of the lucky few that the Louvre allows to copy a painting. But make no mistake, I wasn't a copyist like George. I copied to learn. George copied to create."

Ava's face showed her confusion.

"To outsiders, it looks the same. But there's a world of difference that only an artist can see. If you'd seen George's work, you'd understand."

"How long has Marina taught drawing?" Ava asked.

Apple drew a sharp breath. "Don't ever let her hear you say that. Marina doesn't teach drawing. To use her own words, she facilitates artists in their relationship to drawing."

"What does that mean?"

Apple laughed. "It means that most people are unable to pull out a sketch pad and draw in the Louvre. It can be very intimidating. Passersby peer over your shoulder and expect to see incredible sketches. When people draw in a group, each individual is invisible. Being invisible makes it easy to draw. That's what Marina discovered, and that's what she sells."

Apple stopped speaking and eyed Ava as if she wanted to ask her something. Ava suspected that the woman wanted to know how well she knew George. After all, if Ava had had a brief fling with George, she wouldn't have announced it at the service yesterday.

Suddenly, tears welled up in Apple's eyes.

Ava was concerned. "What's wrong?"

Apple's face was now a mask of sadness "I haven't slept since George died. I keep expecting him to appear and tell me that it was all a mistake… that another George Starr died." She shook her head in disbelief. "People don't die from falling down stairs."

Both women fell silent. When they reached ticket control, Apple flashed her museum pass. Ava showed her journalist's card.

Seeing the card, Apple raised her eyebrows. "You're a journalist?"

"If you call writing tweets and Facebook posts for famous actors journalism, then, yes, I was. Right now, I'm here in Paris taking a well-earned break from being on-call twenty-four hours a day, seven days a week."

"I always suspected that actors didn't do their own social media," Apple said. "I just never thought I'd meet the person who did it for them."

"And now you have."

Apple stared directly at her. "How long have you been in Paris?"

This was the same question Laura had asked Ava at the church. Ava wasn't surprised by it. George must have been meeting someone from London.

Before coming to the Louvre this morning, Ava had decided not to mention that she was a bookseller. For the rest, she'd stick as close to the truth as possible. "My uncle has an apartment in Paris. He's not there now so I come and go."

"That's the ideal situation."

"Coming and going?" Ava asked.

Apple let out a sigh. "Paris is very small. Sometimes, I think I see the same people every day. In fact, I do see the same people every day. It would be nice to get away from them all..."

They frayed their way through the crowds. Ava followed Apple who moved through the packed galleries like a fish in water. She led them to an elevator that was discreetly placed in a side hall.

"The Louvre's elevators are its best kept secret. They whisk you back and forth in time. You can be looking at art from the early middle ages. Then you get in an elevator and you'll have moved two hundred years forward in time when you step out," Apple said.

They took the elevator up. Its doors opened near the Café Mollien. Stepping out, Apple took a few steps and froze. She began to shake.

"I don't know if I'm ready to see where George died."

"Were you here that day?" Ava asked.

"No," Apple said. "George didn't tell me he was coming. He must have been meeting someone."

Ava remained silent.

"Was he meeting you?" Apple asked in a rushed tone.

Ava shook her head. "No. It was only by chance that I read about George's death. To be honest, I'd only met him once. He made a tremendous impression on me. I imagine he had lots of friends he might be meeting."

Apple was disappointed by Ava's response. "George was

very charismatic. He found it easy to meet people. In certain ways, George would have been very pleased by his death."

Ava raised her eyebrows, astonished. "Pleased?"

"A death in the Louvre. It didn't go unnoticed. George made headlines. Maybe not in the way he wanted... He would have appreciated the irony of the situation. He finally became famous and wasn't around to enjoy it."

The two women walked slowly over to the staircase where George had fallen to his death. The crowds of people gaping at the body had vanished. Apple and Ava were the only two peering down at the landing.

"He died here?" Ava asked in an attempt to hide that she had witnessed the death.

Apple leaned over the railing and pointed at the landing below. "Just there."

Unable to stop herself, Ava looked down. To her relief, there was no sign that George Starr had died there. It looked like an ordinary landing in the Louvre. Watching the excited tourists troop up the stairs, Ava felt sad at how quickly George's death had vanished, swept away by the stream of life.

Looking down, Apple stood there for an eternity. When she turned to Ava, she wiped a tear off her cheek. "At least, there's some consolation..."

"What's that?"

"We know it was an accident. No one would murder someone in plain daylight in the Louvre."

Ava remained silent. When she glanced up, she glimpsed the woman who had screamed two days ago staring at her like she had seen a ghost. When Ava looked again, the woman had vanished into the crowd.

Ava had to stop herself from running off in search of the woman. She couldn't do that with Apple at her side. What Ava could do was etch the woman's likeness into her mind so she could find her later.

Ava closed her eyes to "see" the woman. As the woman's face appeared in Ava's mind's eye, she realized why the woman's face had looked so familiar… It was because the woman looked exactly like her!

CHAPTER 9

Pale and on the verge of collapse, Apple moved away from the staircase where George Starr had taken his last breath. "Would you mind if we skipped drawing today?"

Anxious to find the screaming woman, Ava agreed immediately. "I was going to suggest the same thing."

After one last glance at the staircase, a cloud passed over Apple's face. "George's death will always be with me."

Ava choked back a sob. She would never forget his death, either.

Apple and Ava retraced their steps to the elevator and took it down to the lower level of the Denon Wing. As they made their way to the exit, Ava scanned the crowds for some sign of the woman. Once again, she had vanished.

Profoundly troubled, Apple had to sit down several

times as they made their way to the exit. When they reached the glass pyramid, they took the steep escalator to the top. Ava stood behind Apple, worried that she might keel backwards and fall.

As Ava looked down at the atrium, she reproached herself for not noting the resemblance between her and the woman earlier.

How hard was it to recognize your double?

That must be the reason George had come over to the table!

George thought that Ava was the woman he had gone to the Louvre to meet. Given that the woman was ten to fifteen years older than her that meant that George hadn't seen the woman in a long time.

Stepping out of the Louvre's main doors into the bright sunshine, Apple headed to the marble ledge that rimmed one of the outdoor fountains that surrounded the glass pyramid. She sank down onto its solid surface and ran a hand through the pool of water behind her. She rubbed her wet palm on her temples. Ava sat down next to her.

After a long silence, Apple spoke. "I'm sorry. I didn't think it would affect me so much."

"George's death was a tragedy," Ava replied, mouthing the platitudes that people say when someone has died. As a person who loved words, Ava realized that there were times when words were insufficient. What words could possibly capture the horror of George's death?

Apple choked back a sob. "What am I going to do now?"

Knowing there was no answer to that, Ava remained silent.

Apple looked up at Ava. "There are a lot of people I'd like to see dead, but George wasn't one of them."

That statement so astounded Ava that she almost asked who those people were. Wisely, she bit her tongue. There would be time to get that information later.

Ava's goal in coming to the drawing class had been to learn more about George Starr and why he was murdered. Seeing the screaming woman at the same staircase where George had died was proof that there was a link between the two. Now, she needed to discover what Apple knew.

In a way, Ava was better off that Marina had not come today. While Marina might have a lot to say on the subject of George's death, Ava suspected that Marina would have won any war of wits between them. Apple, on the other hand, was on the edge of a nervous breakdown and seemed like a better candidate to pump for information. Ava pushed aside her scruples about preying on Apple's distress... Solving George's murder was more important than anything else.

Peering at Apple from the corner of her eye, Ava wondered what had happened since they had last met. The

Apple she had seen the day before at the St. Roch Church had been distraught, but the Apple who had greeted her this morning had been shaken to the core, and that was before they had visited the spot where George had died.

Something had happened. Ava had to discover what that was. Before she could decide just how she could do that, Apple turned to her.

"Why don't we go somewhere and have a coffee?"

Ava jumped on the invitation. "The Café Marley?" she suggested, pointing at the trendy upscale café located under the arcades of the Richelieu Wing of the Louvre.

Instantly, she regretted the suggestion.

On a day like today, the café would be packed. Being surrounded by chattering tourists taking photos was not the sort of atmosphere that would induce someone to spill their heart out.

"I'd prefer something quieter," Apple replied. "The Galerie Vivienne is behind the Palais Royal Garden. It's beautiful out today so there won't be many people inside."

The Galerie Vivienne was a covered passageway near the Palais Royal Garden and the National Library. Built in 1823, the passageway was gorgeous. It had a glass rotunda, tiled mosaic floors and was decorated in a classical Neo-Pompeian style, complete with ornate marble statues.

"That sounds perfect," Ava replied. "I'd prefer

somewhere quiet, too."

"And far from the scene of the crime," Apple said, rising to her feet.

Scene of the crime... Hearing those words, Ava felt a shiver run up her spine. Did Apple suspect that there was more to George's death than she was admitting? If so, why hadn't she said anything?

Ava followed Apple through a passageway and out onto the rue de Rivoli. They crossed the busy street and headed toward the Palais Royal Garden entrance that was next to the *Comédie-Française*, the French National Theater.

Stepping through the garden's tall iron gates, they strode past the sculpture installation in the first courtyard where black and white columns of different heights rose from the ground in a grid-like pattern. To Ava, the columns looked like remnants of a past civilization rising from the depths of the earth.

The main garden was tiny and more intimate than the Tuileries Garden. It consisted of four double rows of chestnut and lime trees, two on each side of the central space. The trees shaded the elegant arcades of the former palace that now housed shops and restaurants. The leaves on the trees were trimmed to form a wall of greenery from one end of the garden to the other. Formal rose gardens were set around an enormous fountain that was in the center of the garden.

Parisians and tourists sat in the green metal chairs that were scattered about.

"I love the Palais Royal Garden," Apple said. "I often have lunch here when I'm copying at the Louvre. It's so peaceful."

They skirted around a group of older men playing *boules*, the French game where you hit metal balls with another metal ball.

Apple slowed and watched the men. "George used to play with them. He was horrible at the game. The men liked him so much, they always let him play."

The more Ava heard about George, the more she liked him, and the more she regretted his death. Her Uncle Charles had played *boules*, and he had also been a terrible player, although he never would have admitted it.

"Are you from Paris?" Ava asked Apple.

Apple laughed. "No. If you were French, you'd hear my accent. I'm from the south of France. From Nice."

Ava nodded. Nice was where George Starr had lived before coming to Paris.

"I've been here almost two years. It seems longer. I'm a child of the sun. The grey winter days are not easy."

"Where do you live in Paris?" Ava asked.

"In the Beehive," Apple said.

Ava was puzzled. *La ruche*, or Beehive, had been an

artists' residence in the Montparnasse neighborhood of Paris from 1850-1934. Famous artists, from Diego Rivera to Modigliani, Brancusi and Soutine, had lived there.

Seeing Ava's expression, Apple shook her head. "Not the original one, of course. George knew an elderly widow in Nice who had a building in the Marais neighborhood. The building had been empty for years. He convinced her to rent it to him so he could set up an artists' collective. He called it the Beehive. He was on the point of buying the building when he died. Now that he's dead, who knows what will happen?" Apple's face clouded over.

"Do you live there?" Ava asked.

"Marina and I live there in our studios. Two of the men you might have seen at church, Enzo and Marc, also have studios there. Enzo lives in his. Marc lives elsewhere. He comes and goes whenever he feels like working," Apple said, shaking her head in disapproval. "In my opinion, Marc Jardin isn't an artist. He has talent but no discipline. Without discipline, talent means very little."

Ava made a mental note of Marc's last name as she and Apple exited the garden through another large wrought iron gate.

They climbed up a short steep street and crossed over the rue des Petits-Champs that ran in front of the Galerie Vivienne. When they plunged into its covered arched passageway, Ava was astonished by the change in the atmosphere. They had entered a world where everything was filtered and soft. The passageway was elegant and calming. It was like stepping into another century.

Immediately, Apple relaxed. "I'm glad we came here. It was a mistake to go to the Louvre, but I had to do it."

There were two cafés in the passageway. The first café hadn't opened yet. Tables were already set up for lunch at the second one.

Apple slid into a chair at a table in the passageway. Ava sat across from her. French jazz wafted out from the café's interior.

A hipster waiter appeared and handed them menus. "Lunch won't start for an hour. It's just drinks and desserts now."

"Earl Grey tea," Apple said.

Ava frowned, studying the menu. "I want something more bracing."

"English Breakfast tea?" the waiter suggested.

"That sounds good." Ava looked up at Apple. "Are you getting anything to eat?"

Apple shook her head no. "I haven't felt like eating since George died. The pastries here are wonderful."

"*Gateau au chocolat,*" Ava said, despite the fact that chocolate cake at this hour of the day seemed especially decadent.

Apple smiled sadly. "*Gateau au chocolat* was George's favorite."

Ava fell silent. Her path and George's kept coming together in strange ways.

The waiter shifted from foot to foot. "Milk, lemon?"

"Both," Apple replied.

"Both for me, too," Ava told the waiter who vanished as quickly as he had appeared.

"I can never decide. It's only when the tea is in front of me that I know what I want," Apple explained as she played with a blue ribbon wrapped around her wrist.

Ava glanced up. The passageway was almost empty. It was time to find out what Apple knew. Running her mind over ways to get information from her, Ava decided to chitchat her way there.

"Why did you come to Paris?" Ava asked in her opening bid.

"Because of George. We were a couple before. We're not now. I mean, we weren't when he died. We're just friends," Apple replied in a pained voice

"I'm sorry. I didn't know."

"How could you? In any case, we haven't been together since we moved to Paris. George was incredibly interesting and loved people. Don't be fooled, Ava. He spoke to you because you're pretty. George had an eye for women. And they liked him back," Apple said with an indulgent smile that didn't hide her pain. "Women would come and go, but George was always faithful to the important women in his life. He admired our talent and promoted it."

Ava noticed the use of "our".

Apple glanced nervously around. She leaned over toward Ava. "Were you the person George was meeting the day of his death?"

Ava stifled a gasp. "Me? No... I already told you that I only met him once."

Distraught, Apple tried to find the right words. "When you appeared in church, we... I... assumed it was you."

Unwilling to let this opportunity for information slip by, Ava went for the jugular vein. "Why do you believe that George was meeting someone?"

"He told me he was meeting someone who could help him... I just didn't know who or when."

"Help him with what?"

Apple shook her head. "Don't worry. We'll figure it out. I'd hoped you were that person."

Suddenly, Ava realized that Apple's presence at the Louvre had been a pretext. Rather than Ava being the spider pulling Apple into her web, she had been pulled into Apple's web. "Is that why you came to the Louvre today?"

"Yes," Apple said, adding quickly. "I needed to know."

The waiter arrived with their tea and Ava's chocolate cake.

Contrite, Apple smiled a wan smile. "Let's start over. I should have been honest with you instead of trying to trick you. I apologize."

A wave of guilt swept through Ava. She hadn't been honest, either.

"When did you learn about George's accident?" Ava asked, careful to use the word "accident".

Apple bit her lip and sat back in her chair. "One of the curators called me. We know them all."

"I didn't understand what you meant earlier when you said that George was a special type of copyist," Ava said as she poured tea into her cup.

"George was more than a copyist. He worked hard to discover the secrets of the paintings he copied."

Secrets of the paintings... Was that why George had been killed? Ava wondered.

"The Louvre only accepts 150 copyists per year. The museum lends us an easel and our seat. We bring our paints and supplies," Apple said in an animated tone, clearly happy to change the subject. "As an artist, George had a problem. Technically, he could do anything. He just couldn't decide what to paint. It wasn't that he didn't have enough imagination, it was that he had too much imagination. Becoming a copyist was his salvation. Plus, he got to meet people. One of the hardest things about being an artist is the solitude."

"Why are you a copyist?" Ava asked, trying to understand the woman in front of her.

"It nourishes my art. It helps me find solutions for problems I encounter. You don't learn to paint a tree by looking at a tree. You learn to do it by looking at paintings of trees. Every artist solves the problem of putting a tree on canvas in a different way. It's fascinating. When you copy a painting, you enter another artist's personal world."

"Wasn't Renoir a copyist?" Ava asked as she bit in to her chocolate cake. It was sweet, ridiculously rich and delicious.

"Yes, like Degas, Matisse and so many others. Copying was important to earlier artists. Back then, to learn technique you went to the source. It was the only way to dialogue with a work. Today, there are so many other resources available for artists."

"You're a painter?" Ava asked between bites.

"I'm a digital artist," Apple replied. Seeing the astonished expression on Ava's face, she shook her head. "I know. I don't look like a digital artist. Computers are my preferred medium. But my work as a digital artist is informed by classical art. Hence, my life as a copyist."

"What type of art restoration does Marina do?" Ava asked.

"She's specialized in old masters. But she does a little bit of everything."

"Is Laura a painter?"

Apple burst out laughing. "Laura's an artist's best friend and worst enemy... She's a gallerist."

Ava was curious to learn more about Laura. "Does she represent you?"

"Me? Laura worked with famous artists: artists whose work sells. I'm not in that category. Laura didn't choose the artists the gallery represents, they were chosen by the gallery's owner. She just runs it."

"Was she close to George?" Ava asked, hoping that her question wouldn't offend Apple.

Apple sipped her tea and fell silent for a moment, looking for the right words. "Laura knows how to attract men. She's very seductive. But then George knew how to attract women. In their case, it's hard to know who seduced who first. I imagine they'd both claim the honor." Apple put her cup down. "You don't know me. There's no reason for you to trust me. But George asked you to come to Paris because he thought you could help us."

"But I already told you..."

Suddenly, Enzo appeared. He strode up to the table.

"Will she help us?" Enzo asked Apple.

Apple shook her head. "It's not her."

"Of course it's her," Enzo said. He eyed Ava. "We need your help. A car drove straight at Marina and Laura yesterday evening as they crossed the street. It swerved at the last minute. If it hadn't, they'd be dead."

Apple paled. "Marina didn't tell me that. Why would someone want to hurt them?"

Enzo frowned. "You'll have to ask George that." He turned to Ava. "Will you help us or not?"

"I only met George once," Ava protested.

"What are we going to do now?" Apple asked Enzo in despair.

"Muddle ahead. That's all we can do," Enzo replied. "I promise that I'll find a solution."

"Why won't you help us?" Apple asked Ava in a pained voice.

"I'm not who you think I am," Ava protested.

Enzo stared down at Ava, his dark eyes flashing with anger. "I think you are."

Ava flinched when he made a menacing move toward her.

Apple grabbed his arm. "That's enough, Enzo! Even if she is the person George was meeting, there's no reason for her to help us. George is dead, and Ava doesn't know us.

Why should she trust us? And maybe, just maybe, we're wrong, and she's not the person we think she is."

Enzo snorted. "Maybe she is and doesn't know it." He turned to Ava. "We're holding an open house tomorrow night at the Beehive. A night of art. From 7 P.M. to midnight. Come by and join us. Maybe we can convince you then."

"Is that a good idea?" Apple asked.

"Probably not. But it's the only idea I have," Enzo said. He handed Ava a flyer with a beehive drawn on it. An address in the Marais neighborhood was written on the bottom of it.

As Ava took the flyer, a shiver ran up her spine.

George's death would not be the last one.

She hoped she was wrong.

CHAPTER 10

Shaken to the core, Ava watched Apple and Enzo leave the Galerie Vivienne. She looked at the flyer for the Beehive's open house.

What have you done, Ava?

The situation was complicated. Now, she had gone and made it worse. Why hadn't she stated categorically that she was not the person George had gone to the Louvre to meet?

A little voice in her head answered her question...

"Sometimes sleuths have to take risks."

This little voice, what Ava thought of as her "sleuthing voice" was going to take some getting used to. It might even take some reining in unless she wanted to end up dead.

Ava took a last bite of her chocolate cake, looking for

some solace in sweets. However, she now found the chocolate cake cloyingly heavy and sickeningly sweet. With a sigh, she put her fork down and took a sip of her tea. The caffeine gave her just the jolt of energy she needed.

She sat back in her chair and examined what she had learned. No one had ever said that sleuthing was easy. If criminals continued committing crimes, it was because so many of them got away with it.

Her Uncle Charles had once told her that getting away with minor crimes often gave criminals a sense of impunity that led to bigger ones.

Was George's murderer the one who had tried to run down Marina and Laura?

Ava finished her tea and left.

She exited the Galerie Vivienne, crossed the rue des Petits-Champs and wandered down to the Palais Royal Garden. Unable to still her racing mind, she sank into a green metal chair in the shade of a lime tree and took out her phone.

There was only one person who could help her... Henri.

Before she could dial his number, she saw that she'd received a text message from him. It read:

Lunch at 12:30... Café across from Hotel Drouot.

Great minds did work together!

The Hotel Drouot was a French auction house that auctioned off everything under the sun, from mismatched silverware to priceless paintings. It was one of the oldest auction houses in the world.

Reading Henri's message, Ava's gloom lifted.

If Henri was at Drouot, he was onto something.

A text consisting of a single rose emoji from Benji made her smile. Given his love of ancient manuscripts, he would be excited when he learned about George's mysterious sketchbook. He would be less excited when he heard about the memorial service that she had failed to mention she was attending.

Ava checked the time. It was too early to meet Henri, and she didn't feel like going to her stand. She opened a search engine on her phone and typed in 'Laura Gossal art gallery Paris'. Immediately, hundreds of results appeared.

Ava clicked on a photo of Laura at a gallery opening. It was the Delavine Gallery in the 6th arrondissement. It was located on the rue des Beaux-Arts, a street that ran directly to the Beaux-Arts Academy. It was close to her stand and a fifteen-minute walk from the Palais Royal Garden.

Ava stood up and walked back through the garden. She barely noticed the play of sunlight through the trees or the shouts of children as they splashed water on each other from the huge basin in the center of the garden.

She was lost in her thoughts.

George had been dead for over forty-eight hours. The

chances of solving the crime diminished with each minute. Time was of the essence.

Determined, she crossed the rue de Rivoli and went through the Richelieu Passageway to the Louvre Pyramid. From there, she made her way to the Pont des Arts Bridge. She crossed over it, turned right and walked to the Quai Malaquais. Her stand and Hassan's were both shuttered. Ava stopped and ran her hand over her wooden boxes. Their solidity comforted her. George might be gone, but she was alive and had her stand.

Suddenly, something struck her about her conversation with Enzo and Apple: neither one suspected that George had been murdered.

In addition, Enzo was positive that she was the woman that George had been meeting. Had Enzo seen George talking with her or the woman who looked like her?

A more disturbing thought occurred to Ava.

What if Enzo had killed George and was trying to learn if she had seen him at the Louvre? If that were the case, she was in danger.

Disturbed, Ava left her stand and walked up the rue de Seine and turned onto the rue des Beaux-Arts. The Gallery Delavine was in the middle of the street. Its lights were off. It was still closed.

Frustrated that the gallery was closed, Ava was also relieved. She had no idea what she would have said to Laura if it had been open. Ava headed to a café at the top of the street. She ordered a coffee and took a seat at a window, positioning herself so she could see anyone who entered the gallery.

She didn't have long to wait.

She'd barely had time to sip her coffee when Laura walked past with a young woman. When they reached the gallery, Laura unlocked the door. The two women disappeared inside. Seconds later, an angry looking Marc Jardin stormed past the café toward the gallery. Reaching it, he peered in through the front window and went inside.

Seconds later, he and Laura were back out in the street. They were arguing. To be more specific, Marc was arguing as he was doing all the talking. He waved his arms in the air, red-faced. Laura, furious, gripped his arm. She spoke to him. He calmed down and listened, nodding as she spoke. Finally, he turned and strode off in the direction he had come from.

When he went by the café, Ava ducked. She had enough time to notice that his eyes were glassy and that he wove as he walked.

Ava jumped up, paid for her coffee and ran to the door. Before she could leave the café, Laura strode past with an angry look on her face.

Ducking again, Ava's heart began to beat faster. *Something important was about to happen.*

After counting to fifty, Ava stood up and peered out the window. She had a clear view to the end of the street. The moment Laura crossed it and vanished from sight, Ava was out of the café. She reached the corner just in time to see Laura cross the courtyard of the Beaux-Arts Academy and enter its chapel. Ava had no doubts that Marc was inside.

Unsure of what to do, Ava decided to risk following them.

After all, what could possibly happen to her in the Beaux-Arts Chapel in the middle of the day?

As she crossed the courtyard, she realized that George had probably thought the same thing that last day in the Louvre.

When Ava reached the chapel, she pushed the outside door open and went in. She was in small entry hall outside the chapel. Moving forward, she opened a second door and peeked inside.

The chapel was silent.

No one was in sight.

Weighing what to do, she took in her surroundings. The chapel was a disaffected chapel that was filled with copies of famous sculptures that art students in the 19th century had used for inspiration. The statues had been put there at a time when travel was arduous. If you couldn't go to Italy and Greece to see art, art from Italy and Greece would come to you.

Cautious, she advanced slowly. There was no sign of Laura and Marc. As she crept forward, the sound of whispering voices wafted to her from the front of the chapel. Ava kept close to the large modern sculptures that filled the central space, an exhibit by a French contemporary artist. The sculptures were massive and made of metal. Their size hid her presence.

She inched forward slowly, more frightened that she would ever admit.

When she reached the front of the chapel, she peeked out. Marc and Laura were arguing in front of a marble nude. Marc was pacing back and forth like an enraged animal ready to devour its prey. "I need the painting. I have to have it."

"If I had it, I'd tell you. It would solve all our problems, not only yours. But I don't have it," Laura said, exasperated.

Marc balled up his fists. "I'm warning you. I'm desperate. He's threatening to turn me over to the police if I don't pay him."

"Whose fault is that?" Laura asked Marc as anger flashed across her face.

Marc's fury vanished. He hung his head. "It was an accident."

"I know," Laura said in a mechanical voice as if she'd heard this before.

"I'm so scared. I don't know what to do," Marc whimpered.

"Find the painting, and I'll help you sell it. I can't do more than that." Laura walked up close to Marc and stared directly at him. "Someone tried to run Marina and I down last night... You wouldn't know who that was, would you?"

White-knuckled, Marc gripped the base of the marble statue. "It wasn't me! Why would I hurt you? You're the only person who can help me."

Laura stared at Marc and sighed. "I will help you. Just don't come to the gallery anymore."

"I won't," Marc said. In despair, he began to sob. "I didn't mean to kill him. It was an accident."

Ava reeled back in horror. Marc had killed someone! Was it George?

"I'm not going to prison. I'll kill myself first!" Marc said.

Laura stared at him. "Of course, you're not going to prison. We'll solve this."

"Thank you," Marc said with a whimper. "I miss George."

"I miss him, too," Laura replied.

Marc's expression softened. "I'm sorry, Laura. I'm flipping out. George said he'd help me, and now he's dead. Do you think my blackmailer killed him?"

"No. Blackmailers want money. George's death was an

accident... Unless you know something you're not telling me…"

Stunned, Marc shook his head. "I don't know anything about George's accident."

Laura stared at him. "I hope that's true."

She turned and walked off. Marc ran after her. As they passed by Ava's hiding spot, Laura slowed. "You are not to come to the gallery ever again... Is that clear?"

Marc hung his head. "I won't. I promise."

Ava remained hidden until she heard the chapel door slam. Only then did she step out of her hiding place. Trembling, she walked over to a chair and sank down onto it.

Marc Jardin had killed someone!

The idea that Marc had killed someone was utterly preposterous… Yet, he had just admitted his guilt.

Moreover, someone knew about it and was blackmailing him.

Ava quickly realized that the person Marc had killed couldn't have been George as George had promised to help him with the blackmailer.

Ava wanted to dash out of the chapel, but she feared Marc might still be in the courtyard. She waited twenty minutes before she felt safe enough to leave the chapel.

Never had twenty minutes gone by so slowly.

As she sat amidst the modern metal sculptures and the

classical marble statues, the French saying *"jamais deux sans trois"* ran through her mind.

Never two without three...

There had been two deaths, and there would be a third unless she and Henri discovered what was going on.

CHAPTER 11

The taxi sped up the busy rue Montmartre as it headed north toward the 9th arrondissement. Ava was so preoccupied by what she had heard that she barely noticed the driver accelerating, decelerating and braking, as he sped across Paris like a Formula One race car driver nearing the finish line. Normally, she would have insisted he slow down. Today, she ignored the dangerous driving. She also ignored the radio that was blaring out a political talk show that the driver, a red-faced man in his forties, argued with as he drove.

These minor annoyances were unimportant.

All that mattered was reaching Henri.

The faster she spoke with him, the faster they could discover what was going on.

When, brakes squealing, the taxi pulled up in front of the

café across from the Hotel Drouot, Henri was seated exactly where she had expected him to be... at an outdoor table next to the café entrance.

Instantly, Ava felt safer.

Impatient to tell Henri what had happened, she paid the fare and added a large tip.

What did money matter when people were dying, right and left?

Ava stepped out of the taxi and walked toward Henri. Seated at the round marble-topped bistro table, he was scrolling through his phone. Dressed for the warm weather, he was wearing a long-sleeved white cotton shirt with its sleeves rolled up and impeccably cut khaki trousers. Black suede rubber-soled loafers completed the outfit.

Ava's eyes filled with tears as she walked toward him. Next to her late Uncle Charles, Henri was the person who knew more about everything and anything than anyone else she had ever met. He had a deep insight into people's psyches, including her own. Henri would help her separate the chaff from the wheat in everything she had learned that morning.

Seeing her arrive, Henri stood up and kissed her on her two cheeks in a "*bise*", the traditional French greeting. He wiped a tear from her face with his finger. "There's nothing to be upset about. I ordered us some *charcuterie* and cheese," Henri said, pointing at a wooden tray of cold cuts that were in the middle of the table.

Ava was about to say that she was too upset to eat but knew that Henri would not understand that. If he were to face a firing squad tomorrow, he would already be planning his last meal.

The waiter arrived and placed a cheese platter on the table.

Maybe Henri's attitude was contagious because Ava momentarily forgot about Marc, Laura and Apple as her taste buds sprang to life. Ava had a special weakness for cheese. France had over 350 varieties of cheese. Each variety had its own sub varieties. All in all, there were over 1000 French cheeses, and Ava intended to taste them all before she died.

She winced at her unfortunate choice of words.

"Their cheese is excellent. You won't be disappointed," Henri said.

"Is that goat cheese?" Ava asked, pointing at a white log-like cheese.

Henri nodded as he settled back into the red and yellow wicker bistro chair. "*Une bûche de chèvre.*"

Ava eyed the round cheese with a white crust. "Camembert?"

Henri nodded. "Made from raw milk."

Frowning, Ava eyed the other two cheeses. They would test her knowledge. One was a yellowy-white cheese shot through with veins of blue and green. It was definitely a blue cheese.

But from where?

Ava eyed the Hotel Drouot. The workers who transported the goods at the auction house were known as the "Savoyards" as the original workers had come from the Savoie region in Auvergne.

"*Bleu d'Auvergne*," Ava announced.

Henri's eyes twinkled. "To think six months ago, you couldn't tell your *chèvre* from your *Reblochon* ... And the last one?"

"Too easy. It's Emmental."

"From the French Alps," Henri said proudly.

Ava took a piece of bread from the basket and spread goat's cheese on it. As her taste buds savored the cheese's nutty sharpness, she almost forgot everything that was bothering her.

Almost... But not quite.

The memory of the crazed look in Marc's eyes as he spoke about killing someone was impossible to forget.

Henri sipped his wine. "Now tell me what happened. I can see from your face that you learned something incredibly important."

Ava leaned forward in her chair. "Marc Jardin, the man who applauded at the memorial service, killed someone and is being blackmailed."

Henri was so startled that he put his wine glass down. "George?"

Ava shook her head. "No. Before his death, George had promised to help Marc deal with his blackmailers. I can't believe that Laura, who is now helping Marc, would do that if he'd killed George. She's devastated by George's death."

Henri put some cold cuts on a piece of bread. "Why don't you start at the beginning? That way, I can get a better picture of what happened. When we last spoke, you were meeting the Russian artist, Marina, at the Louvre for a drawing class."

"That seems so long ago."

Henri smiled at Ava. "I'm a bit old school on these things. Perhaps I'm too methodical. But I like to hear things in order. I'm also much older than you, and my mind isn't as agile as yours. Plus, we French are less prone to hopping back and forth in a story like you Anglo-Saxons. So, if you could start at the beginning that would help."

"If anyone has a mind that can hop, no... leap, even fly, it's yours, Henri. But I'll try to be more methodical," Ava said, taking a sip of wine.

"Thank you," Henri replied.

"Apple met me at the Louvre. Marina wasn't there. We learned later from Enzo that someone had tried to run her and Laura down last night. Strangely, Marina didn't tell Apple about the accident. I also discovered that George and the others had a problem. I don't know what it was. Apparently, George had gone to the Louvre to meet someone who could help him. Apple and Enzo believe that I'm that person. In fact, Enzo is convinced I am."

"Did Enzo say why he thought it was you?"

"No. He implied that he knew it was me. For a brief instant, I thought that he had killed George and was testing me to learn if I had seen him."

"And now?"

Ava shook her head. "Enzo isn't a murderer. I almost forgot, I saw the screaming woman…"

For the second time, Henri appeared surprised.

Ava could see from his reaction that the woman's reappearance was not something he had anticipated.

"She was at the Louvre eyeing the spot where George died. There's something else that's strange, Henri. She looks like me. She's ten to fifteen years older than I am. But we're the same height and build and have the same heart-shaped face and the same hair."

"So if George hadn't seen her in years, he might have thought you were her from afar?" Henri mused.

"Absolutely…"

"Was the woman alone?"

"Yes. But before I could speak to her, she vanished. I couldn't follow her as I was with Apple."

"Could the woman have followed you to the museum?" Henri asked taking a piece of *charcuterie*.

"No. I hope not," Ava replied, troubled by the idea that someone could have followed her without her noticing.

"What was Apple's reaction when she saw the spot George died?"

"She was devastated. She was so shaken that we left the museum immediately. I was shaken, too. It was like reliving George's death a second time."

"How did Enzo enter the picture?" Henri asked, squinting in the sunlight.

"Apple invited me to the Galerie Vivienne for coffee. It was a ploy to ask me to help her. She must have told Enzo where she was going."

"So Enzo knew that Laura and Marina had nearly been run over but Apple didn't. That's strange."

"I thought so, too. I believe that Apple and Marina had planned from the start to quiz me on what I knew. Perhaps Marina was so shaken by her brush with death that she didn't feel up to coming. But why wouldn't she tell Apple about the car?" Ava asked as she cut another piece of goat cheese and spread it on her bread.

"Marina doesn't trust Apple," Henri said.

"I only met Marina for a few moments. She seemed tougher than Apple. Maybe she was afraid that Apple would crack under pressure. I'll learn more tomorrow when I go to the Beehive." Ava handed Henri the flyer. "Enzo insisted I come. He thinks I'll change my mind if I go there."

Henri studied the flyer and poured each of them more wine. "How do Marc and Laura fit into the story?"

"Apple told me that Laura worked in a gallery. As it was too early to meet you, I decided to go there. It's the Delavine Gallery on the rue de Beaux Arts."

Sipping his wine, Henri listened attentively.

"I went to the gallery. It was closed. I stopped for a coffee down the street. Just as I sat down, Laura arrived. Then Marc appeared. They argued outside the gallery. Marc left. Minutes later, Laura left the gallery. They met in the Beaux-Arts Chapel."

"You followed them there?" Henri asked, frowning.

"Yes. But they didn't see me. I hid behind some large sculptures and was able to hear most of their conversation. Marc was frightened and angry at the same time. He begged Laura to help him. His blackmailers are pressuring him for money. Obviously, Laura knew about it as she didn't ask him who he had killed, nor did she seem surprised when he talked about the blackmail attempt."

Henri sipped his wine.

"Laura didn't appear to be very enthusiastic about helping him, but she said that she might be able to get him money by selling a certain painting."

"Which painting?"

Ava shrugged. "I don't know."

"Is that all they said?"

"Marc said he'd kill himself rather than go to prison."

Henri remained silent.

Ava sipped her wine and cut off another piece of goat cheese. Sitting there in the sun, everything she had just said seemed preposterous. "Marc doesn't have it in him to kill someone."

"I only saw him once, but I agree with you," Henri said. "But that doesn't mean he's not a murderer."

Hearing that, Ava felt uneasy.

"People kill other people by accident or out of anger…" Henri cut off two pieces of Emmental. He put one on Ava's plate and the other on his own plate. "To sum up, Marc killed someone. He gets blackmailed. George said he'd help him. In addition, George had his own problem. George asked someone for help. The person was coming from London. Apple, Enzo and Marina think that person is you."

"And Laura and Marina were nearly run over," Ava added.

"And Marc is terrified that his blackmailer will turn him

in to the police. Which of course he won't."

Ava popped the Emmental cheese into her mouth. "Why wouldn't he?"

"Because that means the blackmailer won't be paid."

"There's something else I forgot to mention. Apple used to be George's girlfriend. They split up when they moved to Paris," Ava explained.

"And Laura?"

"Apple was torn between whether George had seduced Laura or Laura had seduced George. She warned me that George probably would have tried to seduce me, too."

Henri took a piece of ham and placed it on his bread. "George Starr was a charming good-looking man. I can see why women would have found him attractive. I wonder where the screaming woman fits in. It's curious that the three of you all went back to the scene of the crime."

Ava gave a sigh of satisfaction. "Finally, you're admitting that George Starr's death was a murder."

"It's not what I say that's important. It's what the facts point to. From what I've learned since we've seen each other, your initial suspicion might be right."

Breathless, Ava gripped the table. "What have you learned? Tell me."

"First, tell me how Marc was acting when he and Laura left the chapel?" Henri asked calmly. He had an expression on his face that said no amount of begging would get him to say a word before Ava had finished her tale.

With a sigh of impatience, she plunged back into what she had seen in the Beaux-Arts Chapel. "Marc was upset. He was either drunk or high when he arrived there. I imagine that he's going to keep drinking or getting high until he pays off the blackmailer."

"Neither Laura nor Marc saw you?"

"No. I waited twenty minutes before leaving."

"That was wise," Henri said.

Ava cut herself a piece of the Bleu de Auvergne cheese and placed it on a crispy piece of bread and ate it. She washed it down with another sip of the light red wine. "George had a problem. I don't know what it was, but it affected the Beehive. Apple said that he intended to buy the building. Now that he's dead, she doesn't know what's going to happen."

Henri nodded. "Property."

"Property," Ava confirmed.

As a former notary, Henri had a theory that the French killed because of money or passion... Or both. In this case, property meant money.

"Do you think Apple killed him?" Henri asked.

Ava was astonished. "George? Because of the other women? I don't think so. She said he was loyal to the women who counted in his life…"

"Until he wasn't," Henri replied. "It's strange that no one believes that he was murdered."

"Do you have any idea who Marc killed?"

Henri nodded. "I do. I'll tell you about it after we go to Drouot. There's something there I want to show you."

Ava glanced up as the waiter appeared with fresh strawberries and cream. To her delight, he put them down on their table.

After finishing their lunch with strong double espressos, Henri and Ava strolled across the street and entered the Drouot Auction House through its large glass doors.

"What do you know about Drouot?" Henri asked Ava as they crossed the crowded entrance where potential bidders were paging through documentation on items in the upcoming sales.

"I know it's an auction house. When I first came to Paris and heard "Hotel Drouot", I thought it was a hotel," Ava admitted.

"*False friends* can get you into trouble," Henri said with a knowing look. "I learned the hard way that "*une jolie femme*", a beautiful woman, is not a jolly woman in English."

"Hotel was the trickiest for me," Ava said, thinking back to her early days in France. It had taken her a while to understand that the *Hôtel de Ville* was the mayor's office and that the *Hôtel-Dieu* was Paris's oldest hospital. To confuse matters even more, sometimes a hotel was a hotel.

With a sigh, Ava followed Henri up an escalator and through a maze of rooms filled with objects that were up for auction. He slowed when he reached the last room. He headed directly to the far wall where a drawing was hanging. The drawing was under glass.

Ava approached it and studied it. The drawing had different versions of hares and hunters drawn on it. Ava caught her breath. The hares and hunters in the drawing looked exactly like the hares and hunters in George Starr's notebook.

Ava leaned forward to see the auction number. "It's object 152."

Henri opened the auction catalog he was holding and paged through it. He stopped at object 152.

"A preliminary sketch by Lucas Cranach the Elder, 1472-1553. The drawing is thought to be a sketch for the missing painting "Hares Roasting Hunters", also known as "Hares and Hunters". Work sold by the estate of Nicolas Delavine."

Ava's eyes opened wide in astonishment. "Delavine? The same Delavine as the gallery?"

"The very same," Henri said as he examined the drawing.

"The drawing is remarkable. But then the drawings in the sketchbook are also remarkable."

Suddenly, Ava realized what the words in the catalog meant. "Wait a minute. It's sold by the estate of Nicolas Delavine! That means…"

Henri nodded. "Nicolas Delavine is dead. He died two months ago. He fell and hit his head at home. The autopsy showed he had taken heart medication and had drunk quite a bit. The combination made him woozy. He fell and hit his head on the edge of a marble table. His housekeeper found his body the next day."

Ava stared at Henri. "Marc?"

"Unless we find a third dead man, I assume this is linked to Marc. The death was ruled accidental. Nicolas had quite a reputation for drinking."

"What are we going to do, Henri?"

"Try and discover the truth."

"Shouldn't we go to the police?" Ava asked.

Henri eyed Ava. "And tell them what? That we suspect George Starr was murdered? Or that you overheard Marc say that he'd killed someone? He and Laura would both deny it. We can't even use George's problem as a motive as we don't know what that problem was."

Ava was horrified. The room began to spin around her. She felt sick. "We have to do something. We can't let a murderer get away with murder."

"Unfortunately, people get away with murder all the time. But I agree, Ava... We have to do something. But first, we need more information. Ali called a friend of his, Leo Montaigne. Leo's an art advisor. He's also an intermediary, a go-between. He helps people sell expensive works that they might not want to sell at an auction house."

"Like stolen art?"

Henri shook his head. "He's an intermediary not a fence. Sellers often try and hide art from wives or the tax authorities. Art is a high-priced commodity today, a commodity that attracts all types."

"What about a fake? A copy?" Ava asked. She pointed toward the drawing on the wall. "Do you think this is fake?"

"I'm no expert. I'm sure the experts at Drouot have reason to believe that it is an authentic sketch..."

"But you're not sure?" Ava asked.

"I'm no expert..." Henri said. "Another question... Was Apple upset when she spoke about George and Laura's relationship?"

Ava pursed her lips and thought back to their discussion. "She seemed to accept it as "George being George"."

Henri nodded but didn't say anything. Ava wondered what that meant.

CHAPTER 12

A quick taxi ride had whisked Henri and Ava from the busy
9th arrondissement to a spacious penthouse apartment in the
upscale 7th arrondissement near the Eiffel Tower.

Leo Montaigne's assistant ushered them into a large
room with dark red walls. Its thick damask drapes were
closed tightly, and its walls were filled with valuable paintings.
The paintings were hung with little thought as to order,
height or even period. Despite the treasures on the wall, the
room was welcoming.

Henri strolled around and examined the paintings. He
shook his head in admiration. "I had no idea that a treasure
trove like this existed."

"Let's keep it that way," Leo Montaigne, a large, rather

rumpled looking man in his early forties with an easy smile said, waving his hand at the paintings. "Most are only here for a short time. I try to enjoy them while I can."

"Ali said you might be able to tell us about George Starr and Nicolas Delavine," Henri said as he settled into a red leather armchair across from Leo's desk. Ava remained standing.

"So sad... Two utterly stupid deaths. But then death is not always intelligent, *n'est pas?*"

"In my experience, it never is," Henri replied.

Leo snorted. "Spoken like a true notary." He turned to Ava. "French notaries know all the secrets of death. When we die, their work begins..."

Leo settled his large frame into a chair behind his desk.

"What I'm telling you is strictly confidential," Leo said. His eyes showed that he had no tolerance for fools. "But Ali wouldn't have sent you if he didn't trust you," Leo said.

Ava felt that his message was more for her than Henri. The two men had gotten on famously from the minute they had met.

"A notary turned bookseller and detective... I respect that. I started as a surgeon. After one year, I gave it up and turned to art. Life takes us places we never would have suspected," Leo said, philosophical. He leaned over his desk toward Henri. "Can I see it?"

Henri nodded and took George's sketchbook out of a bag. Leo put on white gloves to page through it. Slowly, he moved from sketch to sketch as Ava and Henri watched.

While Leo examined the sketchbook, Ava eyed the paintings on the walls. She wasn't an art expert, but she recognized some of the artists. The paintings were worth a fortune. Yet, Leo didn't seem the least bit impressed by that.

With a sigh of admiration, Leo closed the sketchbook and placed it in the center of his desk. "These drawings are marvelous. Whoever did them captured not only Lucas Cranach the Elder's style but also the very soul of his work."

Ava caught her breath. *Wasn't that what Apple had said about George's copies… that they captured the soul of the painting he copied?*

"I went and saw the drawing at Drouot this morning after Ali got in touch with me about your sketches. It might be a coincidence that it's for sale now. However, I don't believe in coincidences."

"Nicolas Delavine's estate is selling it. What can you tell us about him?" Henri asked.

"Nicolas was a charming scoundrel, and he ran a good gallery," Leo said, settling back in his chair. "Although I never had dealings with him."

"When did Nicolas die?" Henri asked.

"Seven or eight weeks ago. I don't remember the exact

date. He'd been killing himself with alcohol for years. Unless you knew him you wouldn't know he was drunk. He held his alcohol well. What a waste..."

"Tell us about how his estate came to be selling the drawing?" Henri asked.

"There are two Nicolas Delavines," Leo said. "There was the Nicolas who championed unknown contemporary artists. Even when their works didn't sell, he stuck by them. He trusted, that in time, they would become famous. But in the interim he had to live..."

"From what I learned, Nicolas lived well," Henri said with a knowing smile.

"There was the duplex apartment on the Seine. A *riad* in Marrakech. And a palace in Venice on the Grand Canal. Not to mention his expensive tastes for his own art collection, two ex-wives, numerous ex-girlfriends that he was very generous to and his globetrotting. Nicolas used to get up in the morning and decide to go grouse-shooting in Scotland that afternoon. And like that, he was off. To his everlasting disappointment, Nicolas had not inherited a fortune like many art dealers had. He had to find a way to pay for his lifestyle and finance his gallery."

"Forgeries?" Ava asked, trying to piece the puzzle together.

Leo was taken aback. "That's a term I would never use.

That's implying Nicolas knew that the works he was selling weren't authentic. Let's say that he worked with art of unknown provenance. Some would be less charitable and say he sold fakes, but you'll never hear that from me."

"Wasn't Nicolas involved in a scandal a while ago?" Henri asked.

Leo nodded. "For years, Nicolas carried out his "side" business without a hitch. But when he began to sell paintings that were rarer and more expensive, he stepped on some toes. He cut middlemen off from their fees. As a middleman, I assure you that leads to bad blood. Three years ago, he sold a 17th century painting to a Russian businessman. He had two excellent expert opinions authenticating it. But an art advisor that Nicolas had cheated out of fees dropped hints that led the Russian to become suspicious. The Russian had the paint analyzed. They discovered that some of the pigments used weren't available until the 19th century. Nicolas bought back the painting. It was hushed up. Not many people knew about it."

Henri smiled. "But you did…"

"Let's just say I'm curious, and I like to find out what's going on around me. By the way, Nicolas managed to resell the very same painting to another collector who was less curious about its provenance."

"Nicolas must have done well to live like he did," Henri

said.

"Outside of Paris, Nicolas had a good reputation."

Henri turned to Ava. "Leo means that it wasn't a Parisian dealer who was going to take Nicolas down. Honor among thieves..."

Leo burst out laughing. "I didn't say that. You did. In our business, you have to keep your eyes open. But sometimes the prize is so tempting that people close their eyes."

"What about money laundering?" Henri questioned.

"If you want to launder money, art is one way to do it. If you live in a country and are worried that the government might try and take your money from you, art is a good place to park it. There are entire warehouses filled with paintings that the owners put there immediately after buying them. Because of that, it surprises no one when a painting is sold by an unknown collector. Nicolas even sold a painting to a major British museum last year. His star was rising. It's too bad he died when he did. Who knows? He might even have added a penthouse on Central Park to his property collection had he lived."

"Can I venture a guess about the museum painting? Was it by Lucas Cranach the Elder?" Henri asked.

"Yes, it was," Leo replied, poker-faced.

Henri pursed his lips. "Were there any doubts on the painting's authenticity?"

"In the end? No. There were some suspicions in the beginning. The painting underwent all sorts of tests. It passed them with flying colors. But now after seeing those drawings, I suspect it was a fake. Nicolas had found the Holy Grail... " Leo said.

Henri raised his eyebrows, puzzled.

"Someone who had the talent and technical knowledge to do perfect fakes. You need to understand that once a sale is final it's in no one's interest to discover that it is a fake. No museum wants the world to admit they were duped."

"Any doubts on Nicolas's death?" Henri asked.

Leo shook his head. "None. An accident. It was inevitable. He was drinking himself to death... Most evenings, Nicolas was falling over drunk by 6 P.M. And if it was murder, it only sped up his demise by a few months. His doctors had told him that his liver was shot."

Ava leaned forward. "What about Laura Gossal?"

"She still runs his gallery, doesn't she?" Henri asked.

Leo smiled. "Laura is an intelligent, ambitious young woman. Beautiful and sexy. A dangerous combination."

Ava raised her eyebrows. "Dangerous?"

"From a male viewpoint," Leo replied. "She has it all. Nicolas hired her. They dated. And when his eye began to wander, she found the perfect response to that..."

"Another man?" Henri asked.

Leo nodded. "Exactly. It drove Nicolas crazy that she was seeing a penniless painter."

"George Starr?" Ava asked.

Leo nodded. "George Starr. But Laura underestimated Nicolas. His response was to become friends with George. So while Laura had tried to make Nicolas jealous, Nicolas, in a certain way, stole her new lover from her."

"And then?" Henri asked.

Leo shrugged. "And then nothing... Nicolas died."

"And George died this week," Henri said.

"That does appear to be a coincidence," Leo answered cautiously.

"From a man who doesn't believe in coincidences?" Ava said.

Leo burst out laughing. "You caught me. If Nicolas' death hadn't been ruled an accident then I'd say the deaths might be linked. But that just doesn't seem possible."

"Do you have any idea who would have wanted to kill George or Nicolas?" Henri asked.

"For Nicolas, the knives were out. Whenever there is a lot of money involved, you can expect people to have excessive reactions, but that doesn't lead to murder... Even in Paris. The revenge in our profession is more targeted and, in many ways, more lethal."

"Who runs Nicolas's estate?"

"Before he died, he created a foundation: The Nicolas Delavine Foundation. His lawyer, Etienne Blum, manages it and the estate. Blum is the soul of integrity. There is nothing to see there."

Henri looked disappointed. "I agree with you. Etienne Blum is almost too honest for his own good."

"Spoken like a true notary," Leo said with a laugh.

"What will happen to Laura now?" Ava asked.

"Clearly, the gallery won't continue. She'll have to find something else to do. It's a shame. If he had lived, I don't doubt that Nicolas would have married her. If only to steal her away from George. It wouldn't have lasted, but it would have given her a nice nest egg."

"Did you ever meet George Starr?"

"No. Never. But then *mad dogs and Englishmen...*" Leo turned to Ava. "No offense. George had a reputation for being difficult. He refused to sell his paintings."

"Maybe he did, and we just don't know it," Ava suggested.

"And now we never will," Leo said. He paged through the sketchbook once again and stopped on a drawing of a hare. "*Hares and Hunters* is a mythical painting. A lost canvas from 1545 that is said to show hares catching hunters and roasting them alive. I'd give anything to see it. If you hear about it, let me know."

"Even if it's a fake?"

"Please… "unknown provenance". For a painting like that, collectors are prepared to take risks. So are go-betweens like myself," Leo said as he stood up. His expression showed that the meeting was over.

Henri put the sketchbook back in his bag and followed Leo and Ava to the door. When they reached it, Leo burst out laughing.

"What is it?" Henri asked, puzzled.

"I just may bid on the drawing at Drouot. So Nicolas and I will finally do business together… even if it's from beyond the grave."

Silent, Henri and Ava took the elevator down to the ground floor.

When they exited the building, Ava turned to Henri.

"What are we going to do now?"

"I'm off to London to follow up something I discovered in the sales promise for the Beehive." Henri took two keys out of his pocket. "You might want to stay on Mathilde's houseboat."

"Why?"

"Apple, Enzo and Marina believe that you're the person George was going to meet. I don't doubt others will come to the same conclusion."

Ava slipped the keys in her pocket. She looked at the bag

with the sketchbook in it. "Isn't it dangerous to take that with you?"

"It's safer with me than in Paris. Besides, I'm going to need it." Henri took his phone out and called a taxi. "The taxi will be here in five minutes. What are you going to do this afternoon?"

"Sell books. I may not have a *riad* in Marrakesh, but I do have bills to pay," Ava replied.

Henri burst out laughing. "It's too bad Charlie isn't here to see you... saleswoman and sleuth. He'd be proud."

Ava resisted an urge to smile.

CHAPTER 13

Anyone can draw. It just takes practice.

With Ali Beltran's words as her mantra, Ava spent most of the afternoon at her stand trying unsuccessfully to draw her lawn chair. The rest of the time, her mind kept going back to Marc Jardin's confession and Nicolas Delavine's death.

Now she had no proof that Nicolas Delavine was the person Marc had killed, but it did seem likely... unless there was another dead person close to George that she didn't know about.

However, the theory had several drawbacks.

If Marc had killed Nicolas Delavine, why was Laura helping him? Was she happy to have her ex-lover out of the picture?

Leo Montaigne had said that Nicolas Delavine probably would have married Laura had he lived. If Henri were here, he would say: "*follow the money.*"

Clearly, an alive and kicking Nicolas Delavine was worth more to Laura than a dead one.

Ava sighed.

When you read detective novels, everything seemed so clear. But when you were trying to figure it out on your own, things were a lot murkier.

Still, if both George and Laura had agreed to help Marc pay off his blackmailer that meant that they believed that Marc hadn't intentionally killed Nicolas Delavine.

George Starr's death, however, had not been an accident.

The person who had done intended to do it. That's why George hid the sketchbook... to preserve the evidence. Once she and Henri knew what the sketchbook and the drawing at Drouot meant, they would be well on their way to solving the crime.

"How much is the shepherdess?" a tall thin man said holding out the porcelain statue.

Startled, Ava looked up at the man who was staring down at the drawings in her sketchbook. Ava slammed it shut.

"Twenty-five euros!"

The man frowned. He inspected the statue from every

angle. "That seems expensive. There's only one sheep."

Ava rose to her feet. "That's right. It's a rare piece. Most shepherdesses have two sheep," Ava said, reaching out for the statue.

The man wheeled back, clutching his prize tightly. "Twenty euros?"

Ava shook her head. "Twenty-three. Take it or leave it."

"I'll take it, if you can wrap it up."

Without hesitating, Ava ripped her failed drawings from her sketchpad and wrapped them around the shepherdess. She then put the statue in a bag.

As he counted out euros, the man pointed at her sketchbook. "If you want to learn to draw, go on internet. There are lots of "how to" videos."

Ava didn't respond. Did she look like someone who needed a video to draw?

As soon as the man left, Ava took out her phone and searched for a "how to draw a chair video". There were hundreds of them. Were there really that many people who wanted to draw chairs?

The rest of the afternoon sped by as Ava drew chair after chair. She sold seventeen books, a record for one afternoon.

As she drew one last chair, Ava focused her mind on the case. She hoped that she would learn why George Starr had been murdered at the Beehive tomorrow. Henri had promised to be back from London by then. Together, they would catch the murderer, and she would discover who the woman who looked like her was.

Ava caught her breath.

Could her doppelganger, her double, be the murderer?

Like a rat in a maze, Ava ran over the evidence. She decided that the woman couldn't be the murderer. Ava had no good reasons to back up her conclusion. It was just that it was inconceivable that anyone who looked like her could be a murderer.

Ava closed her stand. She needed to go home, take a shower and get ready for the concert this evening. She also had to pack a small overnight bag for her stay on the houseboat.

Thirty minutes later, Ava stepped out of the shower and shook her wet hair. She pulled the fluffy towel around her.

She had no desire to go to the concert. What she really wanted to do was to stay home and sleep in her own bed tonight. But Benji had bought her the concert ticket, and she had promised Henri she would stay on the houseboat.

Throwing on a pair of jeans, a black lace sleeveless top and ridiculously expensive flat sandals she had bought on sale, she put her toothbrush, some creams, and pajamas in a small shoulder bag. Just as she reached the door, her cell phone rang.

She checked the number, smiled and answered.

"What have you learned about George's death?" Benji asked without even a hello.

"Why do you think I'm working on the case?" Ava asked as innocently as possible.

Benji snorted. "I know you, Ava. You've got sleuthing in your blood. When I didn't hear from you this morning, I suspected you were up to something."

"You spoke to Henri?"

"Yes... But I knew even before he told me."

"You really think I have sleuthing in my blood?" Ava asked, pleased as punch.

"Of course, you do. You're a Sext, aren't you?" Benji said. "Plus, you saved Yves' life."

"Henri and I saved his life," Ava admitted. The Yves Dubois case had been her first -- and until now -- only case.

Catching sight of the time, Ava let out a sigh. "We'll have to talk tomorrow. I have to go to the concert."

"Not before I hear what is going on. Henri was too busy to say much. Besides, there's a concert at the church every Thursday in the summer. Just go next week, give the man at the door your ticket and tell him it was my fault that you didn't go. I have thirty minutes before I have an appointment at the Met to see a rare manuscript, so spill the beans."

"Benji, there's so much that's happened. There's even been a second murder."

"Since George's murder?" Benji asked, alarmed.

"No. It was earlier. Let me go up to the tower room. I'll be more comfortable up there."

The tower room was a small room at the top of a winding staircase in the corner of her apartment. It was an odd addition to the apartment. It was Ava's favorite place to sit in the evening. It was like sitting in the stars as the room was one floor higher than all the surrounding buildings. The tower room held a desk and a large comfortable armchair. Her Uncle Charles had called the tower room the "reflection room" as he had done his best thinking there.

She turned off the lights in the apartment, crossed it and unlocked the door to the tower room staircase. She entered the staircase and locked the door behind her.

The door jam was old.

It was impossible to pull the door tightly shut from the inside or outside. If she didn't lock it, the door fly open and bang against the wall.

"Are you still there?" Benji asked.

"I'm just sitting down in my uncle's armchair."

"Who was the second dead person?"

"Nicolas Delavine. He was an art dealer," Ava said. She continued, telling him everything she had learned. She began with her visit to the Louvre, then moved on to the discussion with Enzo and Apple, Marc's confession, the visit to Drouot, and the meeting with Leo Montaigne. She also told Benji about the appearance of the woman who looked like her. She skipped over the car that tried to run down Laura and Marina as that would only worry Benji.

"This is like a whodunit!"

"It is a whodunit," Ava replied. "Although there might be more than one who."

"Don't take this wrong, Ava. But you have a real talent for finding murders."

"Talent? Are you making fun of me?"

"Not at all. I'm admirative but worried at the same time. Now tell me about the sketchbook. Old documents are my thing. The story of the missing *Hares and Hunters* painting is fascinating."

"Benji. You just said something really important!"

"I did? What was it?"

"The drawing at Drouot was old. Maybe it really is an original. Perhaps the person who made the drawings copied it. But the sketchbook and the drawings in it are new. In fact, the price on the notebook is in euros, and the euro has only existed as a currency since 1999."

"So?" Benji asked in a puzzled tone.

"So why hide the sketchbook? Why bring it to the

meeting? Maybe George wanted to prove that the *Hares and Hunters* painting was a fake?

"There really is a *Hares and Hunters* painting?" Benji asked, exited. "Wow!"

"There must be..."

"But why would George want to prove that it was a fake? Wouldn't he want to prove it was authentic? Wouldn't it be worth more that way? Why would Marc kill Nicolas Delavine for a painting that George had?"

Ava fell silent. Benji was right. It didn't make sense, unless... "Benji, there are two paintings!"

"Two! There's the painting that Marc and Laura are looking for which must be the *Hares and Hunters* painting, and there's the painting Nicolas Delavine was killed for."

"But you said Marc killed him by accident..."

Ava looked for a logical response but couldn't find one. "I admit. It makes no sense. But I'm sure there are two paintings! Leo said that Nicolas Delavine had sold a painting by Lucas Cranach the Elder to a museum. Maybe that's the painting that led to Nicolas' death."

"I looked up George Starr. There isn't much on him on the net."

"That's because he's really George Alistair Montague the 6th."

"You didn't tell me that! A false identity and an

aristocrat? This case is like those Russian dolls that you open up and keep finding smaller dolls inside."

Ava heard a noise. "Wait a minute."

"What is it?"

"The doorbell."

"Are you expecting anyone?"

"No..." Ava responded.

"Whatever you do, don't eat your neighbor's pizza. He won't think it's funny."

Ava burst out laughing. Her door was the first one you saw when you reached the top floor. Pizza deliverymen always tried her door first even though the pizza was for her neighbor. "You ate the neighbor's pizza? You didn't tell me that."

"I paid for it! How was I to know you didn't order it for me? I should have doubted that you wouldn't order a pineapple pizza."

"Pineapple pizza! Really, Benji!"

"What are you and Henri going to do next?"

"Tomorrow night, we're going to an open house at the Beehive."

Benji was quiet. "I don't know if I like that. There's a murderer running around. Maybe even two!"

"Henri and I will be together. We have to solve the crime before the next person dies.

"The next person? Who's that?" Benji asked, breathless.

Ava almost said Marina or Laura. But then remembered she also hadn't mentioned their brush with death to Benji. If she did tell him, he would only worry more. "I have no idea. In Agatha Christie novels, people always drop like flies."

"Somehow, that doesn't reassure me. Listen Ava, I have to go to my appointment."

"I'm being thrown over for a piece of paper!"

"I promise that if you look as good after 600 years, I'll give up manuscripts for you. Don't do anything dangerous."

Before Ava could respond, her phone went off. Usually when she had the low battery sign, she had ten minutes. She sighed. She turned on the light and looked for the charger. It wasn't there.

Suddenly, she heard a series of noises. It took her a few seconds to realize that they were coming from her apartment. Someone was inside it. She doubted it was the pizza deliveryman.

Frightened, Ava scanned the tower room for something to protect herself with. Where was a fireplace poker when you needed it? She picked up the metal desk lamp and crept down the stairs. When she reached the door, she stood there and listened.

She could hear the sound of footsteps and of drawers opening and closing.

Finally, Ava heard what she was afraid she'd hear: the sound of footsteps coming toward the tower door.

Ava raised the lamp high in the air.

When the person attempted to open the locked door, Ava shouted. "Whoever you are, I'm calling the police. Go away!"

There was the sound of running footsteps and a door slamming. This was followed by a long silence.

Too frightened to leave the staircase, Ava sat down on the bottom step with the lamp in her hand.

A loud sound woke Ava. She opened her eyes. She was in the dark, curled up on the bottom step of the tower staircase. A lamp was at her feet.

Her body ached. How long had she been asleep?

In a flash, she remembered the intruder in her apartment. Her every sense alert, Ava sat there and listened. All she heard was the sound of her own breathing.

After an eternity, she picked up the lamp and unlocked the door.

Before opening it, she stopped and listened again. Hearing only silence, she took her courage in both hands and pushed the door open. Cautiously, she stepped out into the dark apartment. The only light was from the moon and stars overheard.

She was alone. Whoever had broken in was long gone.

Still wary, Ava walked over to a floor lamp and turned it on. She then went around the apartment turning on every light until the apartment was lit up like a Christmas tree.

She moved her eyes across the room. Nothing was out of order. Everything looked exactly like it had earlier. There was no trace of the intruder.

If she had gone to the concert, she probably wouldn't have noticed that someone had broken in.

Except that she hadn't gone to the concert, she had stayed at home.

Ava had a flash of intuition.

Of course…

The concert ticket! She had dropped it at George's memorial service. Enzo and the others knew about it. One of them thought she wouldn't be at home and had decided to search her apartment.

But how had the person gotten in? Ava had a security door.

She walked over to her front door.

As she examined it, she saw that the hinges were in place. She must have slammed the door closed without locking it. That meant if the door slammed behind you, you would be locked out if you didn't have the key with you.

Ava had done that once. When the locksmith came, he

had drilled a small hole in the door. He put a wire through it and pulled the latch open.

Looking down, Ava saw a wire on the ground.

She wanted to cry. Her "visitor" didn't even have to break the door down. She had made it easy for him.

Ava double-locked the door. She dragged a heavy chair over and placed it in front of it. If her intruder did come back, she would hear him.

Shaken, she plugged her phone into the charger. It was almost one A.M. It was too late to go to the houseboat. She would spend the rest of the night here.

But first, she had to see what the intruder had discovered about her.

Ava moved through the apartment, trying to put herself in the intruder's mind. As many of the books and all of the record albums belonged to her uncle, the person who had broken would have a very skewed image of her.

When Ava reached the bookcase, she halted.

There was a photo of her Uncle Charles standing in front of New Scotland Yard Headquarters on Victoria Embankment.

She picked the photo up and spoke to her uncle:

"I know. I should have locked the door. Don't worry. Henri and I will find George's killer, and we won't die doing it."

With a heavy sigh, she put the photo back on the shelf.

Whoever had come might guess that Charles had worked for Scotland Yard. As her uncle's death hadn't been in the papers, she hoped that the intruder would think that Charles was still alive. She might be able to use that to her benefit.

She picked up her phone that was charging. She thought of calling Henri.

She decided against it. He would only worry.

Overcome with exhaustion, she walked around the apartment and turned off all the lights. She carried the metal lamp from the tower over to her bed. She went back into the kitchen and grabbed a frying pan and a carving knife. She put them on the floor next to the metal lamp and climbed into bed, fully dressed.

If her visitor did come back, she would be ready.

CHAPTER 14

As Ava climbed up the mountain made of chairs, the
mountain shifted with each step. Terrified, she leapt from
chair to chair, trying to reach to the top before the mountain
collapsed. As she moved, the entire edifice shifted
dangerously. Ava eyed the deep chasm. Grasping the back of
a tall chair, Ava pulled herself up. Just when she reached the
top, there was a roar and a cracking sound and the mountain
of chairs went tumbling down, taking her with it.

Gasping for breath, Ava sat up and opened her eyes. She
was in her bed, fully dressed. A metal lamp was on the floor.
A cast iron frying pan and a carving knife were next to it.

Frowning, she gazed around her apartment.

The armchair that was usually near her bed was propped
up against the front door.

Suddenly, everything that had happened the night before

came rushing back. Someone had broken into her apartment, and she had scared the intruder off.

Of course, they had scared the living daylights out of her first.

Still, the intruder had left when she had threatened him.

Feeling comforted by this spin on a somewhat inglorious incident, she climbed out of bed.

If the person had wanted to hurt her, he wouldn't have come when she was supposed to be at a concert.

Somehow, this line of reasoning was not comforting.

An intruder was an intruder.

You didn't grade them based on the time they broke in. The fact was that someone had been in her apartment! That horrified her.

Ava headed to the bathroom and turned the water on. She took her clothes off and stepped into the shower. She reveled in the hot water running down her back. She wanted to wash away everything that had happened the night before. When she stepped out of the shower, she slipped into a terry cloth bathrobe.

Standing in front of her closet, she chose a pair of gray jeans and a pink ruffled top. She added a pair of flat sandals and a silver sweater. Pulling her wet hair back in a ponytail, she put on face cream and her most expensive red lipstick. She was ready to go.

She eyed herself in the mirror. She looked confident. She tried to convince herself that there was nothing to be upset about.

Yes… Someone had searched her apartment. Any sleuth worth their salt had probably experienced the same thing or even worse.

Ava strode to the kitchen.

There was no sign of Mercury. But his bowl was empty, and the box of cat food was on the counter.

Somehow, she had prepared Mercury's breakfast last night before going to sleep.

Looking at the empty bowl, she was annoyed.

What an ingrate!

He could have waited for her to wake up. Instead, he popped in, ate breakfast and ran off without a hello.

Noticing something on the floor next to his bowl, Ava bent over to see what it was.

It was a pale blue ribbon.

She picked the ribbon up and examined it. A beehive was drawn on it.

Frozen to the spot, Ava clutched the ribbon in her hand. Apple had been wearing a pale blue ribbon around her wrist yesterday. Was Apple her intruder?

Trembling, Ava laid the ribbon on the counter and stared at it. She felt dizzy.

It just wasn't possible that Apple was the intruder!

Out of all of the people she had met at the memorial service, Apple was the one Ava never would have suspected. Did Apple suspect that she had the sketchbook or the painting that Marc was looking for? Is that why she had broken in?

Ava grabbed the ribbon off the counter. The moment her fingers touched it, another thought popped into her head.

Marina had kept Apple in the dark about the car that had almost hit her and Laura. Was that because she believed that Apple was linked to the accident? Perhaps Henri had been right. Apple was angry about the women in George's life and had killed him.

If that were the case, it upped the stakes drastically for this evening's visit to the Beehive.

Realizing her chances of dying were increasing, minute-by-minute, Ava poured a generous serving of dried cat food in Mercury's bowl in case she didn't return. As an afterthought, she put the box on the floor. If necessary, Mercury could knock it over and serve himself.

Suddenly, Ava froze.

Mercury!

He had found the ribbon and had dragged it over for her to find. If it had been next to his bowl last night, she would have seen it.

Mercury was trying to help her solve the case!

Teary eyed, Ava vowed to buy him some deluxe cat food. She might even buy him a new bowl when the case was over... if she was still alive to do it.

With one last glance around the apartment, Ava put the ribbon in her pocket, strode to the door, removed the armchair, unlocked it and stepped out onto the landing. She double-locked the door behind her.

Taking the steps two at a time, Ava headed down to the street. When she reached it, she checked her phone. There wasn't a message from Henri. She wondered what he had discovered. There was no point in pestering him. Henri would tell her what he had learned when he arrived this evening.

Ava walked toward the Seine River. She slowed her pace at the Café Zola. Through the whited-over windows, she could see workers on ladders. Ava was cheered by the thought that it would soon open. If it had been open today, she would have gone in and told her tale of woe to Gerard. He would have consoled with a strong coffee and a treat from the kitchen.

This morning, she would have coffee on Mathilde's houseboat.

Henri would not have moved in, even temporarily, without bringing the special blend of coffee that he had freshly grounded for him at a small neighborhood coffee shop. Ava could almost smell the coffee brewing.

She dashed across the *Quai Malaquais* and stopped at her stand. She checked the padlocks on her boxes to be sure that no one had broken into her them.

The padlocks were fine.

One or two book stands on the quay were already open. There was no sign of Hassan.

Ava walked along the quay, sprinted down the steps to the left of the Arts Bridge and headed directly to Mathilde's houseboat. When she reached it, she leapt from the cobblestones onto the houseboat's deck without the slightest hesitation.

If she had survived an intruder, she could certainly survive a dip in the Seine.

Pulling the gangplank down would take too much time. She was in desperate need of a coffee.

Fraying her way through the plants, Ava took a deep breath. The odor of jasmine, honeysuckle and roses hung heavy in the morning air. She continued to the door, unlocked it and climbed down into the boat.

Whereas the light outside was bright, the light inside the boat was soft and filtered. It flickered as the boat moved up and down on the water's surface.

The boat's interior was spacious. The living room had

wood paneling, brightly colored North African rugs and a comfortable leather couch. Two leather chairs stood next to the couch.

Ava skirted them and headed to the tiny, ultra-modern kitchen. A package of Henri's coffee was next to the Italian coffeemaker. She measured it out, added water and put the coffeemaker on the stove.

As the coffee brewed, she peered out the porthole window that gave onto the river. The water splashed up on it as barges floated by with their cargo. From the boat, the river was at eye level. Seeing swans float by, she waved at them.

When the coffee was ready, she removed it from the stove. Its strong, earthy aroma filled the kitchen. It was just what she needed to start the day.

She put the coffee pot and a cup on a tray and retraced her steps through the boat. She climbed up to the deck and headed to the market umbrella. She placed the tray on a low table and opened the umbrella. Then, she unlocked a wooden box and took out some colorful cushions.

She placed them under the umbrella and sat down. She poured herself some coffee and leaned back, gazing at the jungle of flowering plants with contentment as the boat rocked gently up and down.

If she didn't have a murder to solve, she could have gladly stayed there all day.

"Ava! Ava!" a voice shouted.

Startled, she looked up as Hassan leapt onto the boat.

"How did you find me?" Ava asked.

"Henri said you were staying here." Hassan handed her a bag and a newspaper. "Croissants and the morning paper! We have to make do until Café Zola opens..."

"Sit down. I'll go get you a cup," Ava said, happy to have company. She stood up and went inside.

Seeing Hassan put everything into perspective. It was a beautiful day, and she was having breakfast on a houseboat on the Seine.

Everything was fine. There was nothing to fear but fear itself. However, murder had a strange way of throwing you off your path.

She climbed out on deck and walked over to Hassan. She handed him a cup and sank down onto a cushion across from him.

Hassan poured coffee into his cup. He lifted it to his nose. "Henri's blend?"

Ava nodded. "Henri's blend."

Suddenly, Hassan put his cup down. "Ava, what's wrong?"

Tears welled up in her eyes. "I knew I couldn't fool you."

Hassan stared at her, serious. "I'm waiting."

"Someone broke into my apartment last night."

"While you were asleep?" Hassan asked, worried.

"No. Earlier. I was supposed to go to a concert. I decided not to go and went up to the tower to talk with Benji. I heard the doorbell ring. I thought it was the pizza deliveryman for the neighbor. When I got off the phone, I heard a noise in the apartment. Someone was there. When the person tried to open the tower door, I screamed. The person ran off.

Hassan stared at her. "Did you tell Henri?"

Ava shook her head. "No. By the time I left the tower, the intruder was gone. I was fine..." Ava glossed over that she had fallen asleep. Falling asleep after a break in didn't sound like something a sleuth would do. But fear does strange things to people.

"Did the intruder take anything?"

"No. If I hadn't been there, I doubt I would have noticed that there had been a break in."

"How did they get in?"

Ava sighed. "I'd slammed the door shout. It wasn't locked. Last January, I left the key inside and the locksmith came..."

"And drilled a tiny hole in the door," Hassan said with a knowing look.

Ava nodded. "I feel stupid."

" You shouldn't. Half of Paris probably has a tiny whole

drilled in their door."

"Who do you suspect?" Hassan asked.

"It could be anyone who was at the memorial service. I dropped my ticket outside of the church. It blew away. Enzo brought it back, but the others knew about it."

"Do you think Enzo broke in?"

"I don't know," Ava said. She removed the ribbon from her pocket and handed it to Hassan. "I found this in my apartment."

Hassan took it and examined it. "A beehive? Isn't that the name of the artists' collective that George ran?"

"Yes. Apple had a blue ribbon on her wrist yesterday. I don't know if it's the same one."

"I don't like this, Ava. I don't like this at all. The important thing is that you're fine." Hassan opened the bag he had brought with him and put four crispy croissants on the tray.

"With butter?"

A look of astonishment came over Hassan's face. "Is there any other type of croissant?"

Ava picked one up and took a bite. Immediately, she felt better. Hassan opened the paper. He checked the sports scores.

"France won last night's game! There's hope for us yet." Glancing up, Ava saw a headline on the paper's front page that made her choke. She reached out and grabbed the paper from Hassan.

"What is it?" Hassan asked, alarmed.

Her voice shaking, Ava read an article out loud. "Art gallery break-in in the 6th arrondissement yesterday evening. The Gallery Delavine was broken into. Police are looking for the culprit. No art works were taken. Gallery manager Laura Gossal said that the petty cash envelope was missing."

"Laura Gossal... That's your Laura?"

Ava nodded. "It's my Laura, the same Laura who someone tried to run down two nights ago. The owner of the gallery, Nicolas Delavine, died two months ago. The police think it was an accident, but it was murder."

Hassan stared at Ava in disbelief. "Murder? How can you be sure?"

"I heard the murderer confess," Ava replied.

Hassan poured them both more coffee. "Does Henri know this?"

Ava shook her head yes.

"I spoke with my brother. He told me that you and Henri were meeting Leo Montaigne yesterday."

"We did see him. It's a very complicated story," Ava said. "And long."

Hassan plumped up his pillows, grabbed a croissant and leaned back.

Ava ran over everything she and Henri had learned yesterday. By the end, Hassan's mouth was hanging open.

"Fake paintings, two murdered men and a mythical painting that might exist or might not... You've got a best-selling murder mystery there. It has everything."

"Except clues to who the murderer is," Ava admitted.

"Do you think the person who broke into the gallery is the same person who broke into your apartment?"

"I have no idea. I don't even know if it was Apple or not. But I imagine whoever broke into the gallery was looking for the painting that Laura and Marc spoke about."

"Maybe they thought you had it," Hassan suggested as he broke his croissant in two and ate it.

"Why would I have it?" Ava asked, puzzled.

"Imagine... You met George and became his lover. He told you where the painting was hidden. Then before the two of you could sell it, he was murdered for it. After searching George's studio, the murderer realized that someone else had the painting... You!"

"But I don't have it!" Ava protested. "And I wasn't his lover!"

"Whoever broke into your apartment doesn't know that. And now they've learned you have a link to Scotland Yard..."

'Which either makes me a target or someone to avoid."

"I don't agree with Henri about Marc not being

dangerous," Hassan said, shaking his head. "Not at all."

"What do you mean?" Ava asked.

"From what you tell me, Marc is a drunk, and he's on the edge of a nervous breakdown."

"So?"

"Someone like that is dangerous. You heard him admit murder. What else does know?" Hassan asked.

"Marc is a loose cannon."

"And dangerous to someone," Hassan said. "In my humble nonprofessional opinion, everything hinges on the painting."

"*Hares and Hunters?*" Ava asked.

Hassan nodded. "Which leads to several questions... Is the painting authentic? If not, did George paint it? Or did someone else paint it and not want George to sell it?"

Ava narrowed her eyes, deep in thought. "Apple is a copyist."

"Could it have been painted by one of the others?" Hassan asked.

"If Marc had painted it, he could always paint another one. Marina is an art restorer who doesn't paint."

Hassan frowned. "That leaves Enzo and Apple."

"Or someone we don't know about yet," Ava said.

Hassan poured himself more coffee. "As someone who sells objects, I can tell you that some collectors will do anything to get a special piece."

"Even murder?" Ava asked, shocked.

"Even murder," Hassan said, grim-faced. "Any news from Henri this morning?"

"No. He said he'd be back today. We're going to the open house at the Beehive together."

"That's good. For there to have been two break-ins in one night means that someone is getting desperate. Desperate people do desperate things."

Ava took a second croissant. She wondered what would have happened if the door to the tower had not been locked.

Hassan looked up. "The most interesting element is the woman who looks like you."

Ava nodded. "It's a strange coincidence."

"Aren't you curious to learn who she is and how she's linked to George?" Hassan asked.

Ava raised her eyebrows. "Do you think she's the person who murdered him?"

Hassan shook his head. "Impossible. It's absolutely impossible."

"Why?"

"She looks like you, and you aren't a murderer. Take that as a compliment," Hassan said with a smile and a wink.

CHAPTER 15

"This is not an out-of-print jewel, it's a fifteen-year-old guidebook!" a man in a dark suit protested as he haggled with Ava over an old guidebook. Incensed, he pointed to a section where pages had been ripped out. "And it's missing maps!"

"Vintage is vintage," Ava retorted, annoyed. She grabbed the book from his hands. "Suit yourself. Don't buy it. Someone out there will appreciate its rarity."

Startled by her aggressiveness, the man backed down. "There's no reason to be testy. I was just asking."

Wishing the man would vanish, Ava closed her eyes and blinked. When she opened them, he was still there.

"Fourteen euros?" the man asked, opening his wallet.

"Fourteen euros," Ava responded, resolute.

He handed her three 5-euro notes, eyeing her as if she had just escaped from a lunatic asylum.

Ava rifled through her pocket and took out a euro coin.

The man shook his head and put the book under his arm. "Keep the change. Maybe take a walk. You don't seem like you're cut out for this type of work."

Before she could think of a pithy retort, he was gone.

She leaned against her stand. The man was right. She wasn't in a state to sell books. She needed to think about everything that had happened. There were a lot of pieces that needed putting together before she and Henri went to the Beehive tonight.

She strode down to Hassan's stand. He was sitting on a stool next to it, reading a book on Chinese porcelain.

He smiled when he saw her. "What did you say to your customer? He ran off as if you'd threatened him with eternal damnation."

"*Mea Culpa*. I was completely unhinged." Ava held out a euro coin. "He even left me a tip."

Hassan burst out laughing. "That's a first!" Seeing how downcast she looked, Hassan became serious. "Why don't you go off for a while? I'm here until 1:30. I'll watch your stand until then. If you're not back, I'll close it for you."

Ava smiled at him with true gratitude. "Thanks. I was

hoping you'd suggest that."

Hassan held up his cell phone. "If you need me, I'm here. Just call, and I'll be there in a flash."

"Nothing is going to happen to me. I'm fine. I'm more worried about this evening," Ava said.

"Any word from Henri?"

Ava shook her head. "Not yet."

"If Henri said he'd be there, he'll be there," Hassan said. He stood up and put his book down. "Is the Beehive in the Marais neighborhood?"

"It is. Why do you ask?"

"All the galleries in the Marais are having a special arts night. Many will be open until three or four in the morning. They'll be music, food trucks… Lots of events are planned. The streets will be packed." Suddenly, a worried look spread across his face.

"What is it?" Ava asked, alarmed.

"That's the perfect time for a murder!"

Ava wandered off toward the Arts Bridge. Part of her wanted to go back to Mathilde's houseboat. Looking up, she saw the Louvre on the other side of the river and changed her mind. She would go to the Louvre… back to the scene of the crime.

The Louvre was crowded, but it was not as crowded as Ava

had feared. She headed to the Grand Gallery in the Denon Wing. She went directly to the painting George Starr had been copying the day he died.

The original painting was still on the wall. George's easel and the copy he had been working on were gone. Despite that, Ava could feel his presence.

Had George suspected that someone would try and kill him as he worked on his painting that morning?

Ava thought back to George's painting. He had captured the look of eternal sleep on Endymion's face. While the copy was powerful, it didn't have the weightlessness and genius that the drawings in the sketchbook had. Of course, it might be that the drawings were inspired by Lucas Cranach the Elder and not the painter Anne-Louis Girodet. However, Ava suspected that there was more to it than that.

She walked over to a guard in the corner of the hall. "Could you tell me where the paintings by Lucas Cranach the Elder are?"

The guard took out a smart phone and typed in Cranach's name. "There are several drawings in the Department of Prints and Drawings, but you'll need advance permission to see them. *The Three Graces* and other paintings of his are on the upper level of the Richelieu Wing."

"Thank you," Ava said and strode off. She went down to the ground floor, exited the Denon Wing, crossed through the atrium and went up the escalator to the Richelieu Wing.

When she reached its upper level, she hesitated.

Which of his paintings should she see first?

Ava chose *The Three Graces*. It was a painting that she had often seen reproductions of, so she was familiar with the subject matter.

The Richelieu Wing was almost empty. The deafening din of the Grand Gallery was replaced by rooms that were silent except for a few murmured conversations.

The room with *The Three Graces* was completely empty when Ava reached it.

Ava walked up to the painting and studied it.

The Three Graces was a tiny oil painting on wood. It measured only 19 inches tall and 13 inches wide. Ava had imagined that it was larger. She took a plasticized information card that explained the painting's history from a stand on the wall and sat down on a bench in front of the painting to read it.

Lucas Cranach the Elder (1472-1553) was a German Renaissance court painter. He painted religious subjects and nudes from mythology. As was the custom at the time, he had a studio with other painters who worked for him. Cranach often painted different versions of the same painting.

Ava found that interesting. If you were a forger or

painter of works of "unknown provenance", to use Leo Montaigne's words, it would be useful to copy a painter who had assistants doing different versions of the same work.

Cranach had often gone on hunting trips with his royal patrons. He made sketches and paintings of these outings to immortalize the hunts.

Reflecting on the drawings in the notebook, Ava could almost see the hares and the hunters moving through the dense German forests. It all made sense. Cranach had gone on the hunts with his royal patrons in order to capture them on canvas.

However, the person who had made the drawings in the sketchbook was not Cranach and had not gone hunting in German forests in the sixteenth century.

Ava put the information sheet back in its stand and strode up to the painting to examine it further.

The Three Graces was a subject from Greek Mythology. The three graces were the Goddesses of charm, beauty and creativity. It was a subject that many painters had painted. Botticelli's *Three Graces* was one of the most famous paintings on the subject.

Ava studied the three women. Cranach had imbued them with a singular elegance. Their nudity covered them more than any clothing possibly could. They had ironic looks on their faces as if they'd been caught sharing a joke. Their gestures shared the same "lighter than air" quality that the drawings in the sketchbook possessed.

Frowning, she moved back to the bench and sat down.

What did the painting tell her about George Starr and *Hares and Hunters?*

The Three Graces had been acquired by the Louvre for four million euros. While it wasn't the astronomically high sum that some contemporary art works soared to, it was a significant amount. It was enough money to make forgery worthwhile.

"They're so serene, aren't they?"

Ava whirled around. Marina was standing behind her.

"You came to see the painting?" Ava asked.

"I needed to see a Cranach. He got us into trouble. I wondered if he could get us out."

Ava didn't speak. She waited for Marina to say more.

However, Marina sat down next to her and gazed at the painting, silent.

"Enzo told me that you and Laura were almost hit by a car two nights ago," Ava said.

Marina's eyes narrowed. "If Laura hadn't pushed me out of the way, I would have been seriously hurt."

"Was it deliberate?"

Marina shrugged. "Laura and Enzo think it was. I'm not so sure. Parisians are terrible drivers. They hit pedestrians all the time. It's astounding that more people aren't killed by cars."

"Why didn't you tell Apple about the accident?" Ava asked.

"It would have upset her. She would have jumped to conclusions. Apple is very emotional as you might have noticed."

"I thought Russians were emotional," Ava responded, trying to get a reaction out of Marina.

Marina smiled. "Some are. Just like some English people are good at hiding things with their poker faces. I try and steer clear of clichés. I imagine you do, too."

Touché. Ava winced. Marina had gone for the jugular vein.

"Are you coming tonight? Enzo and Apple told me that they'd invited you."

Ava nodded. "Yes. Will anyone else be there?"

Marina laughed. "Half the Marais… It's an open house. Apple and Enzo will give workshops. Marc might appear, but you never know with Marc."

"Will Laura be there?"

"I have no idea," Marina said.

"Her gallery was robbed last night."

Marina froze. "The Gallery Delavine? Are you sure?"

Ava nodded. "It was in the paper this morning."

"Was anything stolen?"

"The paper said some petty cash was taken."

Marina didn't respond. The expression on her face showed that she didn't believe the robbery was about money.

"Was George killed?" Ava asked.

"Killed? You mean murdered?" Aghast, Marina gripped the bench. "Of course not. Why would anyone kill him?"

"To get the painting?"

Marina's expression changed instantly. "I knew you were the one when I saw you at church. Enzo was sure. Apple had her doubts. George wasn't killed for the painting. Why would someone kill him for it? That makes no sense."

"Maybe the person killed George for what he knew?"

Marina shook her head. "There are things you don't understand. It's not that simple. George wasn't murdered. He fell, died and left us with a mess. Are you coming tonight?"

"Yes."

"Are you still interested in the painting?" Marina asked as her eyes drilled into Ava.

"I'm not the person you think I am," Ava protested.

"You know about the painting," Marina said.

Too late, Ava realized that she had dug herself into a hole. Marina was now sure that she was the person George had been meeting about the painting. Luckily, Marina didn't know that she had been at the Louvre and had seen George fall.

"We'll talk tonight. Don't say anything to the others," Marina warned.

"I'm not the person buying the painting!" Ava protested.

"Of course, you're not. You're representing someone. Come tonight. Invite your buyer. If you're not the person I think you are, you have to help us find that person. George brought you into our lives for a reason."

Before Ava could speak, Marina leaned over and began to shake.

"Are you OK?" Ava asked.

Marina took a deep breath. She sat up and pushed her long red hair behind her ears.

Ava stared at her, uneasy.

"I'm so relieved. I haven't stopped worrying since George died. Now that we've spoken, everything is on its way to being solved." Marina stood up. "Come around 8:30. The others will be giving a workshop. We'll have time to talk. Remember, don't say anything to the others about the painting."

Marina walked off. Ava sat on the bench, paralyzed.

What had she done?

She glanced up at *The Three Graces*. The expressions on their faces seemed to echo her thoughts.

CHAPTER 16

The café in the Tuileries Garden was next to a small pond where brown speckled ducks with bright yellow beaks sunned on rocks. Sparrows flittered down from the trees to steal the breadcrumbs that tourists threw in the water. A fat grey pigeon was perched on the head of a statue in the middle of the pond. It looked like a feathered hat that cooed.

Ava was seated at a table on the water's edge. After her discussion with Marina, she had decided to take the rest of the afternoon off. Since George Starr's death, her life had been a roller coaster ride. Tonight's visit to the Beehive would only accelerate that. What she needed was time to sit and think.

She sighed.

What she really needed was for this case to be over before someone else died.

A bearded waiter brought her salad over and placed it in the middle of the table. He set a glass of *Entre-Deux-Mers*, a light fruity white wine from the Bordeaux region, in front of her.

Ave took a bite of her *Salade Niçoise*. The green beans were perfectly cooked. The anchovy filets were salty and bitter. They were the perfect compliment to the baby potatoes. The salad was garnished with both chervil and parsley, and the vinaigrette had just the right dose of Dijon mustard to wake her taste buds up.

At any other time, Ava would have been delighted with her lunch. Today, she was so preoccupied by what had happened since George's death that she barely noticed what she was eating. Sipping her wine, she wondered when the next shoe was going to drop.

When her cell phone rang, Ava answered it without checking the number. Five minutes earlier, she had left Hassan a message that she wasn't coming back to her stand.

"Hassan? You don't mind closing up for me?"

"I'm sure he doesn't, Ava," Henri said.

Ava sat up straight as an arrow. "Henri? It's really you?"

Immediately, Henri noticed her troubled tone. "What's wrong? Are you OK?"

"No, not really," Ava responded. "So much has happened since yesterday afternoon."

"I'm waiting," Henri responded. "Take your time."

"Someone broke into my apartment last night. I was supposed to be at a concert, but I was in the tower talking to Benji. When the person tried to open the tower door, I shouted, and the person ran off."

"Who knew about the concert?" Henri asked.

"The ticket blew out of my notebook at the memorial service. Enzo caught it. But Laura saw it as did Apple and Marina."

"How did the intruder get in?"

"I slammed the door shut. I hadn't locked it," Ava confessed.

"Something you'll never do again," Henri said gently. "You're fine. That's what's important. Did the intruder take anything?"

"Not that I know of. If I hadn't been there, I doubt that I would have noticed that someone had broken in."

"What were they looking for?" Henri asked.

"As the intruder didn't ransack the apartment, I assume he was looking for information. He saw Uncle Charles's photo in front of New Scotland Yard."

"Was there anything else you noticed?" Henri asked.

"Mercury found a blue ribbon. It had a beehive drawn

on it. Apple was wearing a blue ribbon on her wrist at the Galerie Vivienne. I didn't see a beehive on it."

"But there might have been one," Henri ventured.

"Yes. But I can't believe that Apple broke into my apartment. I know... Love and jealousy are always motives! But I wasn't having an affair with George."

"Apple doesn't know that. If it's not love and jealousy, it might be money."

Frowning, Ava ripped a piece of lettuce from her salad and tossed it to a sparrow that had hopped up on the table. "You mean the painting?"

"Yes."

"Or the sketchbook," Ava suggested.

"I'd file the sketchbook under self-preservation. If George was killed because of it, it had a deeper meaning than money."

"The Delavine Gallery was burglarized last night," Ava said.

"You spoke with Laura?" Henri asked, astonished.

"No. It was in the newspaper. The article said that nothing was taken except some petty cash."

Henri was silent.

"There's something else I need to tell you," Ava said, rolling a black olive nervously between her fingers.

"Need or want to tell me..." Henri said in a knowing

tone.

Ava bit the bullet and spit it out. "Both. I went to the Louvre to see Cranach's *Three Graces*. Marina was there. She thinks I'm the person that George was meeting and that I have a buyer for the painting. She wants to talk to me tonight. Alone. I'm not to tell the others."

"That means she has the painting," Henri said.

"Or she knows who has it."

Henri sighed. "Well, that's one thing out of the way."

"You're not angry?"

"Of course not. How can we solve the case if we don't move ahead?" Henri asked. "It's curious that she asked you not to tell the others."

"I thought so, too. She also insisted that George wasn't murdered," Ava added.

"It's odd that no one thinks George was murdered."

"She even believes that the car that almost hit her was an accident."

Henri's tone became somber. "If she has the painting and isn't the murderer, she's in danger."

"Who do you think did it?" Ava asked as she popped the olive into her mouth.

"It depends on how you define "it". There's the murder, the blackmailer, the break-in to your apartment, the burglary in the gallery and the attempted hit and run… There's something else I need to tell you," Henri said, hesitating.

Ava could hear the change in his voice. Something major had happened. Something dramatic. "What is it, Henri?"

"Claude Monet called me."

A shiver ran up Ava's spine. There was no reason for Claude to call Henri unless something extremely serious had taken place. "What did he say?"

"The river police found a body early this morning in the Seine near the Ile de la Cité. A man…"

Before Henri said the name, Ava knew who it was. "Marc?"

"Marc," Henri confirmed.

"He committed suicide?"

"They're going to do an autopsy," Henri replied "Some homeless people were drinking at the Square du Vert-Galant last night and heard arguing."

The Square du Vert-Galant was situated at the far end of the Ile de la Cité, the island Notre Dame Cathedral was on.

Ava frowned. "Did the people see who was arguing?"

"No. It was dark as the sky was clouded over. When they heard loud voices, they thought it was some drunks fighting."

Ava caught her breath. "So it might be murder."

"Yes," Henri said.

"Does anyone at the Beehive know?"

"First, the police are not sure that the dead man is Marc

Jardin. They based their preliminary identification on the wallet in the man's pocket. When they're sure, they'll contact his family. So no one at the Beehive knows," Henri said. "We can't pretend to know, either. For us, Marc is alive. If hewas murdered, only the murderer would know that."

Stunned, Ava stared at the pond. The stakes were rising every minute. As a duck flew up, flapping its wings and spraying water all around, Ava had another thought. "Marc's blackmailer wouldn't have killed him. If he did, he wouldn't be paid. Marc doesn't have the painting because Marina does. Or, at least, we think she does… "

"Marc's death doesn't make sense to me. But it does to the murderer," Henri said.

"Nothing makes sense, Henri. Nothing."

"Where are you?" Henri asked.

"In the Tuileries Garden having lunch," Ava confessed. "After last night, I didn't feel like working at my stand."

"Whatever you do, don't go home. Go to Mathilde's after lunch and rest. We have a long evening ahead of us. My Eurostar train arrives at 8 P.M. I'll take a taxi directly to the Beehive and meet you at the café on the corner at 8:20."

"What do you think will happen?" Ava asked.

"We'll find out tonight."

"Are you going to be my buyer?"

"I'll be an old friend of George's."

Ava took a sip of wine. "What have you learned in London?"

"Enough to understand that the answer lies at the Beehive. All the suspects will be there."

"Did you find the woman who looks like me?"

"Yes."

Excited, Ava pushed her plate away. "Who is she? What was she doing in the Louvre? Is she coming back to Paris?"

"I can't talk now, Ava. I have one more person to see before I leave. Remember, wait for me at the café on the corner. Do not go into the Beehive without me," Henri said and hung up.

Ava finished her wine and signaled to the waiter. "An espresso... No, make that a double espresso."

Henri was right. It was going to be a long evening.

CHAPTER 17

The party was in full swing when Ava reached the Marais neighborhood. The sound of a trumpet wailed over the deep-throated voice of a jazz singer, belting out old favorites on a street corner. A three-piece orchestra played nearby while people danced in the street. Nearby, other people drifted in and out of art galleries, clutching plastic goblets of wine.

The joyful atmosphere lifted Ava's spirits. However, she was unable to chase away the ominous feeling that had taken hold of her since her talk with Henri.

Three people were now dead -- George Starr, Nicolas Delavine and Marc Jardin, and she had no idea who the murderer was.

Taking Henri's advice, she had spent the afternoon on

Mathilde's houseboat in the shade of the market umbrella. To her astonishment, she had fallen into a deep dreamless sleep. The loud horn of a passing barge carrying sheep down the river had woken her. After freshening up, she decided to walk to the Marais. As she walked along the river, she stopped and stared at the Square du Vert-Galant where Marc's body had fallen into the water.

Murder or suicide?

There was no way of knowing without more facts. It wouldn't surprise her if Marc had been drunk and had fallen in the water. But what was he doing on the riverbank of the Ile de la Cité at night?

Ava reminded herself that, for the others, Marc was alive. She had to be careful not to slip up.

Walking through the carnival-like atmosphere in the Marais, Ava was swept away by the wellspring of energy around her. It drove home to her that life was fleeting. You had to enjoy it while you could.

Taking her own advice, she stopped in a gallery to get herself in the right mood for the Beehive. Unfortunately, the paintings were abstract works in tones of red and black that looked like blood. They reminded her that three people were dead and that she and Henri had no idea who the murderer was.

Exiting the gallery, she sat down on a bench to run over

what she knew one last time.

What had struck Ava from the beginning was that no one at the Beehive appeared to know the whole story. They each knew bits and pieces.

Maybe the murderer knew the whole story... But if that were the case, everything would have ended with George's death, and it hadn't. So there had to be things the murderer didn't know, and that's what was causing the string of deaths.

Laura and George knew about Marc's involvement in Nicolas Delavine's death and the subsequent blackmail. Did anyone else know about it?

Why was everyone so sure that George had not been murdered?

Apple, Marina and Enzo knew that George was meeting someone to help them with their problem. Did they know about his Louvre meeting?

For Ava, the biggest mystery was George's problem. No one had mentioned what it was. Ava found that odd.

She suspected that it had to do with a painting. Was that *Hares and Hunters*? Did *Hares and Hunters* even exist?

Could the Gallery Delavine be involved? Laura had told Marc she would help him sell a painting. Was that painting *Hares and Hounds*? Had Laura taken up the mantle of the late Nicolas Delavine and was now dealing with art of "unknown provenance"?

Henri always said "follow the money". Before he left off to London, he had discovered something in the sales promise for the Beehive. What was that and who benefitted from it?

Then there was Enzo. He puzzled her. Laura had been very touchy-feely with him at the memorial service. Yet, Enzo seemed quite solicitous of Apple at the Galerie Vivienne. Was he a playboy like George? Or was he using the women for a more nefarious purpose?

George had had relationships with many women. Maybe one of them was linked to his death... It might even be the screaming woman from the Louvre.

Ava let out a deep sigh. How on earth were she and Henri going to discover the answer to all these questions in one evening?

If this were an Agatha Christie mystery, it would all unravel neatly like a ball of string.

But this wasn't an Agatha Christie mystery.

Real life was more complicated.

Standing up, Ava frayed her way through the mobbed streets. When she reached the street that the Beehive was on, she slowed.

The Beehive occupied an entire 18th century building on the corner of the street. Its front door was wide open. A pale blue banner with "Open House" written on it was hanging over the doorway. A beehive was drawn in the center of the banner.

There was only one café on the block. It was at the far end of the street where a brass band was playing. Ava checked her phone for the time.

It was 8:15. Henri would be there any minute.

Ava zigzagged in and out of the blocked traffic. The cacophony of honking horns blended into the loud band music. A teen on skates rolled up to her and stopped. He held out a basket filled with pale blue ribbons.

"The Beehive ... Tonight. Be there or *bzzzz*," he said, making a buzzing sound as he handed her a ribbon.

"*Bzzzz*," Ava responded as she took the ribbon.

She strode past the brass band and entered the café. It was a real Parisian café with a zinc bar and small marble topped tables. She chose a table near the entrance and ordered a coffee. She placed the ribbon the young man had given her on the table. She took the ribbon Mercury had found out of her pocket and laid it next to the other ribbon. They were identical.

That meant anyone linked to the Beehive could have broken into her apartment as they all would have had access to the ribbons.

Worried that tonight might not go as smoothly as she hoped, Ava decided to send Benji a text.

It would be an upbeat, cheerful text.

If she was killed, let Benji remember her as someone who was brave and audacious.

Taking out her phone, she typed in: *All well. Solving case with Henri. We'll have our man or woman by dawn.*

She added a heart emoji and hit send just as a text from Henri arrived.

Henri's text was brief: *In taxi. Arriving soon. Have important news.*

Ava's heart skipped a beat. Henri had important news! She hoped it wasn't another death.

Looking up, she saw two people enter the café and head to the counter. It was Apple and Enzo. Both had blue Beehive ribbons around their wrists.

Immediately, Ava grabbed the ribbons, her phone and her coffee. She scooted to a table behind a pillar. She caught her breath and tried to make out what Apple and Enzo were saying. As she listened, she watched their reflection in the plate glass window.

"An espresso," Apple said to the barman.

"Make that two," Enzo added. He turned his attention to Apple. "You've been avoiding me. We need to talk."

Apple sighed. "I'm upset, Enzo. George is dead. We don't have the money to buy the Beehive, and there are things going on I don't understand."

Enzo grabbed her arm. "Why won't you listen to me?"

Apple brushed his hand away. "Because I don't know what you're talking about."

"You're in danger!" Enzo whispered loudly.

"Don't you start, too! Laura insinuated that I was hiding one of George's paintings."

"They'll turn you into Interpol! Is that what you want?" Enzo asked. "They want the painting and won't stop until they get it."

"Who is this mysterious "they"?" Apple asked, annoyed.

"I don't know," Enzo admitted.

"That's what I thought. Let them turn me into Interpol. I didn't do anything. I don't have the painting they're looking for. And even if I did, I wouldn't give it away."

Enzo was so angry his body began to shake. "You're still protecting George. This is his fault. Now that he's dead, they'll discover your role in the paintings."

Hearing the word "paintings", Ava almost fell out of her seat.

She was right!

There was more than one painting.

"I don't know what you're talking about," Apple said as she downed her coffee in one gulp.

"Keep your head in the sand and you'll have problems," Enzo proclaimed angrily. His tone softened. He brushed his fingers over her hair. "I want to help you."

Apple bristled at his touch. "Like you're helping Laura?" She stared at him. "What is it about her that turns men into putty?"

"I'm not interested in Laura. She's George's victim just like you."

Furious, Apple stepped toward Enzo. "I forbid you to speak like that about George." She was so angry that she was about to explode. "Whatever he did, he did for us and for the Beehive."

"Except you're the one who will go to jail," Enzo insisted.

"For what? For loving him too much... for admiring him? If that's the case, I'll gladly go to jail."

"Apple, you have to cooperate..." Enzo said ominously.

Exasperated, Apple sighed. "That's enough. We have a workshop to give."

Enzo threw some coins on the counter, and the two left.

Craning her neck, Ava peered out of her hiding place and watched Apple and Enzo leave the café. They walked through the crowd and disappeared from sight.

She took out her phone and texted Henri: *Where are you?*

"Right behind you," a deep voice said.

Startled, Ava looked up.

Henri was standing next to her. He was wearing khaki

trousers and a white long-sleeved shirt with the sleeves rolled up. He had white sports shoes on his feet.

"Henri!" Ava said. She'd never been happier to see anyone in her life.

He slid into a chair across from her.

"Did Enzo and Apple see you?"

"They don't know who I am," Henri reminded her. "They both had blue ribbons around their wrists."

Ava showed him her two blue ribbons. "The Beehive made them for the open house."

"So that means our proof that Apple broke into your apartment…"

"Doesn't mean anything," Ava admitted, disappointed.

Henri ordered a mineral water. "What were they arguing about?"

"Enzo babbled on about Interpol. He told Apple that she risked going to jail. She didn't appear concerned. In fact, she looked at him like he was nuts. However, when he attacked George, she became angry. Laura was another sensitive topic."

"And Marc?"

Ava shook her head. "They didn't mention him. They must not know that he's dead." She stared into Henri's eyes, uneasy. "Shouldn't we let the police investigate George's death?"

"Investigate what? An accident?"

"Couldn't Claude Monet convince them?" Ava asked.

"That there was a murder at the Louvre on his watch!" Henri said, incredulous. "Can you imagine what that would do to attendance?"

"You're right. That won't work," Ava said. She shook her head in despair. "I keep seeing George Starr appear at our table. We can't give up. We have to solve his murder."

"Who said we're giving up? We will solve it."

Excited, Ava leaned forward. "You know who the killer is?"

"No... But everyone will be there tonight. Chances are that one of them is the killer."

Suddenly, Ava frowned "If Marc was killed that means the killer is desperate. Desperate people do desperate things."

"What better method than to catch the killer in action?" Henri asked.

Ava frowned. "Isn't that a bit risky?"

Henri eyed her. "There's no reason for the killer to kill us. We don't have what he or she wants."

Mollified, Ava sat back in her chair. "Uncle Charles used to say: Never reverse a decision because of fear."

"Exactly," Henri replied. "Giving up would be a betrayal of Sext and DeAth."

"What do we do now?" Ava asked.

"You go to the Beehive first. I'll arrive a few minutes later."

"Who are you exactly?"

"A friend of George's from London," Henri said. Seeing the incredulous look on Ava's face, he burst out laughing. "Surely, if you can be a Parisian, I can be a Londoner."

Wisely, Ava chose not to respond. "What did you discover that was so important?"

"Besides your *doppelganger*?" he asked, referring to the woman who looked like her.

"Besides her," Ava responded.

"George Starr didn't paint *Hares and Hunters*."

Stunned, Ava stared at Henri. "If George didn't paint it, who did?"

"That's what we have to find out."

CHAPTER 18

Pushing through the raucous crowd on her way to the Beehive, one question ran through Ava's mind:

Would she and Henri find the killer before the killer found his next victim?

When she reached the Beehive, its front door was open. She peered in. No one was in sight. The only sound was Enzo's voice coming from the other side of a closed door to the left of the entrance. A "Class in Progress" sign was taped to the door.

Ava entered the building. She glanced right and left. She was alone. She moved to the door with the sign on it and put her ear up against it. She listened for a moment but couldn't make out what was being said.

She turned her attention to the Beehive itself. The

building was from the 18th century and looked it. The paint on its walls was peeling. The wooden stairs that led to the upper floors were worn. The building smelled damp as if there had been years of unrepaired water leaks.

Ava walked up to the wooden table in the entrance and ran her hand through the basket of blue ribbons that was on it.

Marina appeared. She had an unlit cigarette in her hand and looked worried. Seeing Ava, her face lit up. "I was afraid you wouldn't come."

Surprised, Ava pointed at her cigarette. "You smoke?"

"Only when I'm nervous, and today I'm very nervous. I wanted to cancel the Open House. Apple refused." Marina put her unlit cigarette on the table. "I don't light it. That's my compromise."

"Are the others here?" Ava asked, looking around.

"Enzo and Apple are giving a drawing course," Marina said, pointing at the closed door. "As usual, Marc hasn't appeared. Nothing new there. He's totally unreliable."

Ava managed to keep her expression neutral. "Is Laura coming?"

"She said she'd stop by. Her link to the Beehive was George. Now that he's dead, she doesn't come as often as she used to," Marina said.

Marina walked up to the closed door, opened it a crack

and peered inside. Ava sidled up behind her and eyed the interior.

Inside the room, Apple was pointing at a wine bottle on a table. "Don't look at the bottle with your eyes. Look at it with your hand. Close your eyes and let your hand "see" it on the paper."

"Your eyes are the pencil," Enzo added as he walked around the room where fifteen people were drawing with their eyes closed.

Two people appeared at the Beehive's front door behind Ava and Marina.

"Are we too late for the class?" they asked.

Marina shook her head. "No."

She handed them paper and pencils. They slipped into the room.

She closed the door behind them and turned to Ava. "We don't have a lot of time. The class will be over in twenty minutes. Is your friend coming?"

Just as she spoke, a figure appeared in the front doorway. It was Henri. He walked up to Ava and kissed her on the two cheeks.

Turning to Marina, he smiled. "Henri DeAth, a friend of George's from London."

Marina frowned. "He never mentioned you."

Henri was unperturbed by her challenge. "George only

admitted that his London life existed when he needed one of us. I hadn't heard from him in fifteen years when he contacted me out of the blue."

Marina's expression was guarded.

Henri took the sketchbook out of a bag slung over his shoulder. "He sent me this and asked me to come. My train was late. As George, Luddite that he was, said that he didn't believe in cell phones, I asked Ava to meet him. Unfortunately, he died before she arrived at the Louvre."

Marina turned chalk white when she saw the sketchbook. She reached out for it. Hearing Enzo's voice echo from the door behind them, she pulled her hand back. "Put it away. Don't let anyone see it."

Henri slipped the sketchbook back in his bag.

"Do you want to buy the painting?" Marina asked.

"I don't have that type of money, but I know people who do. When I spoke to George, I told him that. But he was so upset, he didn't listen."

Marina shook her head. "I'm sorry George is dead. But he was selfish. He thought he was smarter than everyone else."

Henri nodded in agreement. "Then he hadn't changed. He always thought he was smarter than everyone else. In most cases, he was right."

Marina waved at the steps and started up them. "Let me

take you on a tour of the Beehive."

Ava and Henri followed her.

"The building is unusual. I'm not surprised that George called it *the Beehive*. The winding staircase goes all the way up to the roof. There are five floors. Each floor has two large rooms that give onto the courtyard and two smaller rooms that give onto the street. Many of the rooms are in such bad shape that we don't use them."

"Have you been with George long?" Henri asked.

Marina raised her eyebrows. "I was in no sense *with* George," she said sharply. "I met him right after he opened the Beehive. I was looking for a space to live and work in. The price was right. Although there was always a bit of drama with him."

Ava looked surprised. "Why do you say that?"

Marina rolled her eyes. "George fancied himself an anarchist. He was always thumbing his nose at society. When you're born with a silver spoon in your mouth, that's easy to do."

"Why don't you want the others to know about the painting?" Henri asked.

Marina halted on the third floor landing. "Because they'd complicate things. Apple would get on her high horse, and Enzo is a little too tight with Laura. George wanted to use the money so the Beehive Association could buy the building. I intend to follow his wishes."

"And stay here?" Henri asked.

"A free studio for life is impossible to turn down," Marina responded and headed up to the next floor. "My studio's on the fourth floor. George's is on the top floor."

At the next floor, Marina took a key out of her pocket and unlocked the door at the head of the stairs.

"Did you see the sales promise?" Henri asked.

Marina froze and eyed Henri. "George told us that he put it in the name of the association."

Henri shook his head. "He did. He created another association in London with an administrator there."

Ava's heart skipped a beat. *The administrator must be her screaming woman!*

Marina was shaking in anger. "Will we lose the Beehive?"

Henri narrowed his eyes. "No, I don't think so. I believe he set up another association because he was afraid."

Marina flinched but didn't say anything. Instead, she pushed the door to her studio open and stepped inside. The room was pitch black. Ava and Henri followed her in.

Immediately, Ava was assailed by the odor of oil paint and turpentine.

Marina walked to the end of the room and swung open the shutters. Light filtered in. Paintings hung on the walls. Two paintings were on easels. Marina covered each of them with a cloth. "Sunlight can be fatal for paintings like these."

"You work in the dark?" Ava asked.

Marina shook her head. "No. Sometimes I use candlelight to study a painting. But when I work, I have a special light I use that won't damage the paint."

Ava eyed the paintings on the walls. "Won't they be hurt by light?"

"They were painted with modern pigments that are stable. Hundreds of years ago, painters blended mineral pigment, ash and bone into their colors. The result was often light sensitive."

"What are your conditions for selling the painting?" Henri asked, all business.

Marina didn't hesitate. "It has to go to a private collector, very private. No institutions. No foundations. And no museums."

"Like the first Cranach?" Henri asked.

Marina went white and slumped onto a chair. Henri's words were like a bullet to her heart. "George did talk to you," she said, a statement not a question.

Henri sat down across from her. "What happened?"

"George met Nicolas Delavine. They never should have met."

Henri pursed his lips. "Nicolas Delavine had a reputation for…"

"Finding paintings no one else could. And there was a reason for that," Marina replied.

"How did you meet Nicolas?" Henri asked.

"I restored some paintings for him. He came here to see them. That's how he met George"

"Did Laura come with Nicolas?" Ava asked.

Pretending not to know who Laura was, Henri raised his eyebrows. "Laura?"

"Laura Gossal, the woman who runs the Delavine Gallery. She was seeing both George and Nicolas," Marina explained. Looking at Ava, she sighed. "Unfortunately, Laura came here with Nicolas, and that's how it started between her and George."

"Was she involved with the paintings?" Ava asked.

Marina raised her eyes to the heavens. "No, thank goodness. This was all between George and Nicolas."

"Where did you fit into the picture?" Ava asked.

Marina waved her hand at a palette and brushes "Technical advice. I work with old paintings. I know what paint painters used at each period."

"Why did you agree to help them?" Henri asked.

Marina wasn't surprised by his question. "Greed. It was written in the association bylaws that the original members were given lifetime free access to their studios."

Henri frowned. "What went wrong?"

"Nicolas fell and died."

"Murder?" Ava asked.

Marina eyed Ava. "You have murder on the brain. No, Nicolas' death was an accident. He drank too much. One night, he fell and hit his head. It was fatal." Worried, she turned to Henri. "You don't think that George was killed, do you?"

"Sometimes an accident is an accident," Henri replied.

Marina looked relieved.

"Who painted the painting?" Henri asked.

Marina frowned and eyed him as if she didn't understand the question. "George. Who else?"

"When he spoke with me, he said, "we painted it","
Henri explained.

Marina nodded. "In a way, he was right. For the first Cranach, George took a second rate period copy of a Cranach and turned it into an original. So there were two painters. Three, if you count Cranach."

"In the end, the experts declared that the painting was a genuine Cranach," Henri said.

Marina looked bitter. "Yes. But by then Nicolas was dead, and we still hadn't received all the money."

Henri frowned. "The Cranach was sold last year."

Marina nodded. "Nicolas gave George a first payment when the sale went through. That was what George used to pay the deposit for the Beehive. After that, Nicolas always had an excuse. First, it was liquidity problems. Although that didn't stop him from renovating his palace in Venice... When two experts voiced doubts on the Cranach's authenticity, Nicolas said we had to wait until that played out."

"And now?" Henri asked.

"Now that the first Cranach has been authenticated, I want to sell another Cranach," Marina replied.

"Of unknown provenance."

"Of course. You get what you pay for," Marina replied sharply. Suddenly, her expression softened. "The moral of the story is that you should never trust experts... especially when a lot of money and reputations are at stake."

Henri pointed to the bag on his shoulder "And this?"

"George's sketches for *Hares and Hunters*. He was obsessed with the painting. He talked about it nonstop. He spent years doing research on it. He didn't want to sell it, but it was the only way to buy the building," Marina said with a sigh. "I'll be sad to see the painting leave. But the Beehive is important."

Ava paced across the room, puzzled. "Why didn't you sell it yourself and keep the money?"

Marina appeared surprised. "Because I have no intention of going to jail. Keeping my studio will be enough. I'd also like to know that the painting is in good hands."

"Can we see it?" Henri asked.

Marina nodded. "George kept it in my studio as people were always in and out of his studio." She walked to a door at the end of the room and unlocked it. She turned on the light and stepped inside.

Seconds later, she reappeared. She was white as a ghost and shaking. "It's gone!"

Henri and Ava rushed over.

Barely able to stand, Marina pointed at a shelf. "It was there."

Henri and Ava eyed the other shelves that were empty except for painting supplies and blank canvases.

"When did you last see it?" Ava asked.

Barely able to articulate, Marina stepped back into the studio. "Three or four days before George's death."

Henri helped Marina over to a chair. "Who has the key to your studio?"

" I do. George did. I removed the key from its hiding place in his studio after his death," Marina said.

"Could George have moved the painting before he died?" Henri asked.

Marina nodded. "But why? Where would he put it?"

"In his studio?" Ava asked.

Marina shook her head. "He wouldn't have done that."

"George hid it somewhere. We have to find it," Ava said.

"Do you think one of the others took it?" Henri asked.

"How would they know that it was in my studio? How do they even know it exists?" Marina asked.

Suddenly, Marina's cell phone rang. She answered it and listened. "Calm down. Yes, we're all here. The front door is open."   "What is it?" Ava asked.

Marina looked troubled. "It's Laura. I could barely understand her. Something's happened."

CHAPTER 19

Apple stepped back to inspect the pencil sketches she had just taped to the wall. When Marina came down the stairs, Apple looked at her and pointed proudly at the drawings.

"Look at them. For some of the students, it was their first time drawing! George was right. Anyone can be an artist," Apple proclaimed.

Hearing George's name, Marina snapped at her. "I'm sick of hearing about George."

Enzo strode out of the empty classroom holding his cell phone. He looked troubled. "Laura texted me that... "

"I know. She's on her way here. I just spoke to her," Marina said, shutting down the discussion.

When he saw Henri and Ava coming down the stairs, Enzo stared at them. His troubled expression changed to a hostile one. "And you are?" he asked Henri.

With a broad smile, Henri stepped forward and held out his hand. "Henri DeAth. An old friend of George's."

Apple caught her breath. "From London?"

Henri nodded. "From London."

Enzo crossed his arms and confronted Ava. "If he's George's friend, who are you?"

Henri answered for her. "Ava's a friend of mine. I was supposed to meet George the day he died, but I missed my Eurostar. As George doesn't believe in cell phones, I asked Ava to tell him I'd be late. Unfortunately, he died before she got there."

Apple began to cry softly.

Marina walked over and hugged her. "Tears aren't going to help, Apple. We have to figure out what to do."

"You've come for the painting?" Enzo asked Henri, getting directly to the point.

"Why else would he be here? Certainly not to take a drawing class," Marina replied.

Ava's eyes moved from Apple to Enzo. She wondered if one of them had the painting. She could tell from the expression on Henri's face that he was thinking the same thing.

Striding over to a door on the opposite side of the hallway, Enzo swung it open. "We can talk here. The sooner this ends the better."

Enzo, Apple, Ava and Henri stepped into the room. Marina hung a "closed" sign on the front door and joined them.

The room was a small sitting room. The wallpaper had been pulled off, revealing the cracked plaster on the walls. The furniture was old and covered with large swathes of material. A porcelain parrot stood on a shelf. A table in the corner was set up with chips, cookies, wine and plastic cups.

Apple spoke directly to Henri. "I'm Apple, short for Aphrodite. I see you've met Marina." She pointed at Enzo. "And this is Enzo." Defiant, she crossed her arms and stared at Enzo and Marina. "Let me be clear, I won't permit you to sell any of George's paintings."

"It's not your decision, Apple. George decided to sell the painting before his death. We have to honor his wishes," Marina responded calmly.

Apple's expression showed she wasn't swayed by Marina's argument.

"What did George tell you?" Enzo asked Henri.

Marina sighed. "Henri knows about the museum. He knows about *Hares and Hunters.* And he knows that the buyer has to be discreet. He also knows something that we don't know."

Silent, Enzo and Apple looked from Marina to Henri.

"George signed the sales promise in the name of an association he created in London. It has another administrator. It's not you, Apple," Marina said.

Stunned, Apple shook her head. "That's not possible. I gave George my power of attorney."

Marina pursed her lips. "Which he didn't use."

With a worried look on his face, Enzo spoke to Henri. "Does that mean we'll lose the Beehive?"

"I don't believe so. I don't know all the details. I do know that George did it to protect the Beehive," Henri replied.

"But why?" Apple asked, crushed by George's betrayal.

"Because he didn't trust us. That's why," Marina said sharply. "You spent your whole relationship looking at George through rose-colored glasses."

Apple sank down onto the couch in a daze. "I don't understand."

Enzo glared at Apple, furious. "What's there to understand? George lied to you. He lied to me. He lied to everyone." Furrowing his brow, Enzo spun toward Henri. "If you get the painting, can you guarantee that we can keep the Beehive?"

"Nothing is ever sure… But I'd say your chances are 99%," Henri said.

Enzo looked at Apple and Marina. "Then we all agree?"

"Do we have any choice?" Marina asked.

Apple shook her head. "No, I don't agree."

"But you won't stop us?" Enzo asked.

"How could I do that?" Apple asked, puzzled by his question.

"By keeping the painting!" Enzo replied.

"How can I keep it? I don't have it," Apple said.

Enzo erupted in anger. He clenched his fist and hit it against the wall. "Of course you do. Who else would have it? You need to give it to us. Keeping it links you to the other Cranach, and that's dangerous... more dangerous than you know."

"Cranach!" Apple exclaimed. "What Cranach! What does George have to do with a Cranach? He never painted a Cranach in his life!"

Ava looked at Apple, puzzled. Apple seemed sincere. If Apple hadn't helped George paint the Cranach, then who had? More importantly, who had taken it from Marina's studio?

There was frantic knocking at the front door.

"That must be Laura!" Enzo said. He left the room.

Marina sighed. "There's always drama with Laura."

Everyone fell silent when Laura entered the room. She looked like she hadn't slept. Her features were drawn, and she had dark circles under her eyes. Her curly blond hair was tied back. She was wearing jeans and a T-shirt. Both were wrinkled. It was a far cry from the immaculately dressed Laura who had been at George's memorial service. Laura was so upset, she could barely walk. Tears were running down her face.

Enzo, Apple and Marina were astounded.

"What is it?" Apple asked.

"It's Marc," Laura said in a near whisper as she sank down onto an upholstered stool. "Something's happened to him."

Hearing Marc's name, Marina scowled. "What's he done now?"

Laura shook her head. "No. This time it's serious. He's disappeared." She paused and wiped tears from her cheeks with the back of her hand. "I think he's dead."

"Dead?" Apple went white. "Are you sure?"

"Fairly sure. I can't be certain until the police release his name," Laura said. Looking up, she noticed Henri for the first time. "Who are you?"

"Henri DeAth. An old friend of George's from London."

Laura knitted her brows. For a brief second, her grief gave way to worry.

"You can talk in front of Henri. He knows about the Cranachs," Marina said.

Enzo strode over to the table and poured some wine into a plastic cup. He brought it over to Laura. "Here. Drink some. You'll feel better." He then poured wine into several cups and distributed them to the others. "It was to celebrate our first Open House. Now I suspect it will be our last."

Distraught, Apple rose to her feet and walked over to Laura. "What happened?"

Laura choked back a sob. "It all started with Nicolas and George and the first Cranach they sold."

"First Cranach?" Apple repeated in disbelief.

Laura looked up at Apple. "George didn't tell you he was selling it because he knew you'd disapprove."

Apple's face became a mask of pain.

Laura took a sip of wine. "At first, it was about the money. George wanted to buy the Beehive. He needed money. But then he became caught up in the game of tricking the experts. "A bunch of snooty no-nothings" is how he described them. He delighted in the notion that he could trick them. Instead, Nicolas was the one who tricked George. Instead of selling the Cranach to a private collector as he had promised, he sold it to a British museum. When George found out, he was livid. He was so angry that Nicolas paid him the first installment right away. That's what George used to sign the sales promise."

"That wasn't the Cranach that the experts claimed was a

forgery?" Apple asked.

Laura nodded. "The very same."

Apple looked as if she was on the verge of collapsing.

Laura continued. "When the Cranach's authenticity was called into question, Nicolas used that as a pretext not to pay George the rest of the money. George was philosophical about the situation. He believed he'd get the money sooner or later. He convinced the Beehive's owner to give him an extension on the sales promise. Marc was not as forgiving. He stormed off to see Nicolas at his apartment. They argued. Nicolas was drunk."

"Surprise, surprise," Marina said with cynicism dripping from her voice.

Laura ignored her. "I wasn't there. I'm telling you what Marc told me. When Nicolas tried to throw him out of the apartment, Marc pushed him. Nicolas fell backwards and hit his head on the edge of the marble table. Dizzy, he rose to his feet. He grabbed Marc and tossed him out of the apartment. Unfortunately, Nicolas died that night from the fall."

"Marc killed him?" Marina asked, horrified.

Laura began to weep. "Yes. But it was an accident. I only learned about it after George's death. Marc had no one to turn to. He turned to me. Someone had security tapes from the inside of the apartment and was blackmailing him."

Hearing this, Marina looked puzzled.

Laura turned to Henri. "That's why George contacted you. He wanted to sell the second Cranach to get money to pay the blackmailers."

"But he died first," Ava said as she pieced the puzzle together.

Laura nodded.

Enzo was unmoved by the tale. "Why do you think Marc is dead?"

"He called me last night. He was drunk as usual. He said he was meeting someone who could help him. They were meeting near the Square du Vert-Galant on the Ile de la Cité," Laura said.

It took all Ava's self-control not to react when she heard this. She caught her breath and waited.

"Who was he meeting?" Henri asked calmly.

"I have no idea. I just thought it was the ranting of a drunk. He said he'd call me after the meeting. He never called. I didn't think anything about it. This morning, I went to pick up some paintings that were being framed on the Ile de la Cité. When I stopped for a coffee at the bar across from the Square du Vert-Galant, the barman was talking about a body that police had fished out of the Seine early that morning. The police questioned people in the neighborhood asking if they'd heard a fight the night before. I called Marc immediately. When he didn't answer, I called him again. I left him several messages. I even went to the room he was renting. He wasn't there. An hour ago, my framer called me and said that he'd heard from the river patrol that they found a wallet with a credit card in Mark Jardin's name on the dead man."

The room was totally silent.

Pale, Enzo downed his wine. "You have no idea who Marc was meeting?"

Laura shook her head. "It could have been anyone. Even one of us."

"Why would he meet one of us on the Ile de la Cité? That makes no sense," Enzo said.

"Maybe it was about the painting?" Marina suggested.

"Two people are dead because of the painting. It's cursed," Enzo replied. He turned to Apple. "You have to give it to Henri. He'll help us buy the Beehive just as George wished. And no one else will die."

"I'd give it to you if I had it, but I don't have it. Why won't you believe me?" Apple asked in a high-pitched voice that showed she was at her breaking point.

"Why won't you help us? I don't have it. Marina doesn't have it. Laura doesn't have it. That just leaves you," Enzo said.

"Or George," Marina added. "He might have hidden it somewhere before he died."

Apple stood up and strode to the center of the room. "I have something to tell you about George's death."

Everyone stared at her. The room was so silent you could have heard a pin drop.

'I was at the Louvre the day George died. I killed him," Apple stated without emotion.

Enzo rushed toward her. He grabbed her shoulder and shook it. "Stop, Apple. Stop. I beg of you. I won't say anything."

Distraught, Apple wiped a tear from her cheek. "I knew George was up to something. He didn't tell me what. I only learned about the painting and his Louvre meeting by eavesdropping. I hated myself for doing that. I followed him to the Louvre. I went to the café, and then he fell."

Laura froze and stared at Apple in disbelief. "You were at the Louvre?"

Apple nodded as tears ran down her cheeks.

Ava felt like she was about to burst. Of all the possible suspects, she never would have guessed that Apple was George's killer. Detective novels were right... It's always the one you least suspect.

"You pushed him?" Henri asked gently.

Apple went white. "No. Of course not. Why would I do that? But if George had been able to trust me, he wouldn't have had to sneak to the Louvre where he slipped and died."

Enzo's face showed his relief. "You didn't kill George. It was an accident."

Apple shook her head. "It's all my fault. If I had been less judgmental, George would have told me about the painting. He'd still be alive." Weeping, she ran out of the room.

Laura rose to her feet. "I'll go calm her down. We don't need a third accident." She left the room, closing the door softly behind her.

Enzo strode to the table and poured more wine in his glass. He held the bottle up in the air. "Anyone else?"

Marina raised her glass. "Do you even need to ask?"

Enzo poured her some wine. "Since this seems to be "tell the truth" hour, there are things that Laura didn't tell you." Enzo turned to Marina. "The car that almost hit you? It wasn't an accident. It was a warning."

Marina frowned. "A warning about what?"

"To give up the painting," Enzo said.

Marina remained silent. She stared at Enzo, waiting for him to finish.

"After Nicolas's death, someone called Laura and threatened her. Apparently Nicolas had promised *Hares and Hunters* to someone. We don't know who. They said they'd tell Interpol that George painted the Cranach in the British museum unless they got *Hares and Hunters*."

"Laura told you this?" Marina asked.

Enzo nodded.

Henri's expression was deadly serious. "And then?"

"When Laura told George about the threats before his death, he refused to give her the painting. He said that Nicolas's promises didn't bind him. George even dared the person to turn him in to Interpol. He said that he was proud to have painted the painting. Then when George died, the person became more insistent. There was the car that nearly hit you. This was followed by the break-in at the gallery. I wonder now if George's accident was an accident," Enzo said and downed his wine. "I'm worried that something is going to happen to Apple."

"Apple?" Henri asked with a puzzled look. "What does she have to do with it?"

"We all know that George isn't the genius painter everyone thinks he is. For his copyist work, Apple would do the basic sketches. George would work from those. Even in a painting's later stages, Apple helped him. So no matter how much she protests, she must have helped him paint the Cranachs. He certainly didn't do it alone."

Marina paced back and forth, more and more nervous. "I'm going to go check on Apple and Laura."

Ava stood up. "I left my handbag in your studio. Can I go get it?"

"Of course. It's unlocked. Apple's studio is under mine. Come with me," Marina said.

The two women left the sitting room and entered the entrance hallway.

At the bottom of the steps, Marina turned to Ava. "Now we know that George took the painting."

"Any idea where he would have hidden it?" Ava asked.

Marina shook her head. "None… But there's something else that's bothering me, something that Laura said. I just don't know what that is."

They walked up the steps. When they reached the third floor, Marina stopped in front of a door and knocked softly.

"Apple. Laura. It's Marina."

There was no answer.

Marina knocked again, this time with more force. When no one answered, she opened the door and peered inside. "Apple. Laura!" Frowning, she closed the door. "They must be in the kitchen downstairs. Go on up. My studio is open."

Ava walked up the stairs slowly. She had learned so many things that her head was about to burst. Some things made sense. Other things puzzled her. The only thing she was sure of was that George had been murdered.

Entering Marina's studio, Ava walked around it slowly. She raised the cloth that covered the first painting. Instantly, her eyes were drawn to the tiny section that Marina had restored. It vibrated with intensity.

She pulled the cloth down and went over to the second painting and raised the cloth that covered it.

The painting was almost completely restored.

Once again, life sprang from the canvas.

A shiver ran up Ava's spine.

The paintings vibrated with life. They vibrated just as the drawings in the sketchbook had. Ava wondered if George and Apple had used these paintings for inspiration.

Suddenly, Ava heard footsteps overhead. This was followed by the sound of something falling.

Someone was in George's studio!

Without hesitating, Ava dashed out of Marina's studio and ran up the stairs. On the fifth floor, she threw the door open and came face to face with Marc Jardin.

A Marc Jardin who was very much alive and angry.

Before Ava could react, Marc grabbed her and put his hand over her mouth.

Don't scream or you'll regret it," he threatened, wild-eyed.

In response, Ava bit his hand. Hard. He pulled it back in pain. She picked up a chair and held it high in the air.

"Come one step closer, and I'll scream the house down."

Instantly, Marc's eyes widened. "Don't do that. I don't

want him to find me."

"Who?" Ava asked, keeping the chair high in the air.

"The person who tried to kill me last night," Marc said, shaking. "I need the Cranach. As soon as the person discovers I'm still alive, he'll try and kill me again."

"You have to give me the painting," Ava said. "That way, you'll be safe."

"I don't believe you. But it doesn't matter. I don't have it, and it's not here," Marc said. He sank to the floor and put his hands over his face, distraught. "What am I going to do?"

Ava put the chair down and sat on it. "Tell me what happened last night. We all thought you drowned."

"Who told you that?" Marc asked.

"Laura. She told us about your call last night. That you told her you were meeting someone. This morning, she heard that they found a body near the Ile de la Cite. Your wallet was found on it."

Marc went white. After a long moment of cautious silence, he spoke. "I received a call. Someone said they wanted to see me. They suggested that we could solve my problem without money. They said they'd leave me instructions. I was to wait on the quay below the Square du Vert-Galant."

Ava listened intently.

Marc looked at her and winced. "I know. It sounds like a

bad spy novel. But I was desperate. I waited. No one came. When it got dark, I was leaving. Someone rushed out and pushed me in the Seine. Normally, there would have been lots of people around. But the weather was rainy last night. It was just the local drunks and me. The minute I hit the water, I went under. I didn't scream or splash around. I was worried the person had a gun. I let the current carry me. At the end of the square, I was able to grab a rope from a barge and pull myself out of the water. I was scared. I jumped over the fence and hid in the closed square. I got drunk with some guy who was sleeping rough there. I fell asleep under the bushes. When I woke up this morning, he was gone. My phone and wallet were also gone."

"Did you see the person who pushed you?"

"No," Marc said. "There's something else that's odd. I didn't talk to Laura. How would she know I was meeting someone?"

Stunned, Ava didn't respond. A million theories raced through her mind. The first of them was that Marc was so drunk he didn't remember talking to Laura.

"You're sure you didn't speak to her?" Ava asked.

"I'm sure," Marc said.

"Did you break into the Gallery Delavine or my apartment two nights ago?"

Flustered, Marc stood up. "Why would I do that? I'm in

enough trouble as it is."

Suddenly, Marc froze as the implications of what he said hit him. "Why would Laura lie?"

"I don't know," Ava said truthfully.

Suddenly, Marc's eyes widened. "Last year, we all went to Deauville. It's on the Atlantic Coast. When the others went swimming, I told them I didn't know how to swim. I lied. In reality I just didn't want to go in the water. It was too cold. Laura was there. She heard me say that."

Ava's expression darkened. "If George hid the Cranach, where would he have hidden it?"

Marc waved his hands at the studio. "Here. But I've looked everywhere, and I can't find it."

"What if he hid it somewhere other than the Beehive? Where would that be?"

A shifty look came over Marc's face. "I don't know. I have no idea."

Suddenly, there was shouting from downstairs.

When Ava turned her head toward the noise, Marc dashed toward the window, leapt out and scampered over the roof.

Ava ran to the window. "Marc!"

Marc didn't look back. He continued to run. Several times, he lost his balance and slid down the roof. Each time, he pulled himself up and continued on. For a brief instant,

Ava considered following him. One look down at the cobblestoned courtyard five floors below was enough for her to discard the idea.

As Ava hurried down the stairs, she ran into Henri, Enzo and Marina coming up them.

"Are Laura and Apple up there?" Marina asked.

Ava shook her head. "No. They aren't in George's studio either. I thought I heard a noise. No one was there," Ava said. She deliberately didn't mention Marc Jardin's miraculous resurrection from the dead. If Enzo was in cahoots with Laura, he might have been the one who pushed Marc into the Seine.

In despair, Marina sank down onto a step. "They've disappeared. Where did they go? I looked everywhere. I even called the bar at the corner. They aren't there."

Enzo was beyond panicked. "Maybe the person threatening Laura took them?"

Ava stared at Marina and Enzo. "If George hid the painting somewhere other than the Beehive, where would he have hidden it?"

Enzo shook his head. "There is nowhere else."

Marina spoke. "At the church?"

Enzo stared at her and slapped the side of his head. "Of course, the St. Roch Church!"

"Why there?" Henri asked.

"George was recreating church paintings that went missing during the French Revolution. He'd work on them here but would often finish them in the church."

Suddenly, Marina paled. "Nicolas didn't have a video surveillance system in his apartment."

"You're sure of that?" Henri asked.

Marina nodded. "I worked with him. One night, he tried to seduce me over drinks at his place. I pushed him off and got him talking about his collection. I asked him about security. He laughed. He said with all the shady things he'd done in his life, the last thing he wanted was camera footage that the police could get their hands on."

All four of them stared at each other.

Enzo broke the silence. "I told Laura that George was going to the Louvre that morning. I did it to protect Apple."

Henri's expression was now somber. "We have to hurry."

They dashed down the stairs and stepped out into the street where the party was still in full swing.

Traffic was at a complete standstill.

Enzo used a taxi app on his phone to call a taxi. "There are no taxis available. The fastest way is to take the metro."

Without a word, they all began to run.

CHAPTER 20

The St. Paul Station on the Paris Metro Line 1 was only a fifteen minute walk from the Beehive. Despite the crowds and general chaos in the streets, Marina, Ava, Henri and Enzo made it in ten.

"We're only five stations from the Tuileries Station," Enzo told Henri as they hurried down the steps into the St. Paul Station. "We should be there in six to seven minutes."

As Ava and the others pushed their way into the packed metro car, it was clear that the ride would take longer. With all the shoving and elbowing to get on and off, it took a full three minutes before the doors closed at the St. Paul Station.

Ava was squeezed in the corner of the packed metro car with Henri. Each passing minute seemed like an eternity to her. She glanced over at Enzo and Marina. The crowd had pushed them into the center aisle. Enzo was on his phone. When the pastor of the St. Roch Church had not answered his phone, Enzo had sent him a text message from the platform. Seeing that Enzo was speaking to someone, Ava prayed that it was the pastor.

As the metro pulled away, Ava leaned toward Henri. "Marc is alive!"

Henri jerked his head and stared at her.

"He was in George's studio looking for the painting," Ava said.

"And the river?" Henri asked after a quick glance to ensure that neither Marina nor Enzo was in earshot.

"Someone did push him in the Seine. He didn't see who it was. He was able to climb out. He spent the night in the Square du Vert-Galant."

Henri frowned. "Who is the dead man?"

"Probably the rough sleeper he got drunk with. Marc's wallet and phone were gone when he woke up this morning."

"Why didn't you tell us this back at the Beehive?" Henri asked, knitting his brows together.

"Because Marc said he didn't speak with Laura last night. Maybe he was so drunk that he didn't remember, but I believe him."

Henri's expression darkened.

Ava nodded as if reading Henri's mind. "Exactly. What if Enzo and Laura are in cahoots? What if Enzo pushed Marc into the Seine?"

"Where is Marc now?" Henri asked in a rushed whisper.

"When I asked him if he knew of anyplace George might have hidden the painting, he said no. Then his expression changed. He jumped out the window and ran off over the roofs."

"So he's on his way to the church," Henri said. "If Marc isn't lying, then Laura is dangerous. She's already killed two people."

Ava was stunned. "George and Nicolas!"

Henri nodded. "If we don't stop her, she'll kill Apple."

"Why?"

"Because if I'm right, Apple saw Laura at the Louvre. She just hasn't put two and two together yet."

Ava's expression changed. "So Laura pushed George?"

Henri nodded.

For the rest of the ride, Ava tried to wrap her mind around the fact that Laura was a murderer.

When the doors opened at the Tuileries Station, Henri and Ava pushed their way out and stepped onto the platform where Enzo and Marina were waiting.

Enzo waved his phone in the air. "Father Philippe was having dinner with friends. He's on his way back now. He'll meet us with the keys."

"He's sure the church is locked?" Marina asked in a low voice.

Enzo shook his head yes. "They lock it right after evening mass."

The group came up out of the Tuileries Station on the busy rue de Rivoli. Traffic was at a complete standstill. The sea of cars was surrounded by the sound of honking horns. Motorcycles zipped dangerously in and out of the blocked traffic.

The Tuileries Station was only two minutes from the St. Roch Church. When they reached the Baroque church, its massive blue doors were closed. The small doors to the left and right of them were also locked.

Enzo went up the steps and inspected the small door on the left. He turned to Henri. "Maybe if we fling our bodies against it, it will open."

Henri shook his head. "It will set off the alarm. We don't want Laura and Apple to know we're here."

Enzo's phone rang. He answered and listened, nodding his head. "We'll be right there." He ended the call and turned to the others. "It's Father Philippe. He's caught in traffic. He wants us to meet him at his apartment two blocks away."

"Let's go," Henri said to Enzo.

Ava instinctively understood that Henri didn't want to

leave Enzo out of his sight on the off chance that he was working with Laura.

"Ava and I will wait here," Marina said as she sank down onto the church steps, stricken by the turn of events.

The men nodded and ran off to the left of the church.

"Do you think Laura killed George?" Marina asked Ava.

"I don't know. Why would she do that?"

"For the painting. For the money. The gallery will eventually close. Nicolas Delavine was the Gallery Delavine. Nicolas had no equal when it came to charming birds out of trees and rich buyers out of their money. Laura doesn't possess that type of charm."

"How did George get into the church?" Ava asked.

"He had his own keys," Marina responded.

"Which Laura and Apple must now have..." Ava said.

"That makes sense," Marina replied as she looked out at the traffic in front of the church. "We couldn't have picked a worst night for this to happen."

Ava felt like she was about to explode. "You stay here. I'm going to walk around the building and see if I can discover anything."

"Shouldn't I go with you?" Marina asked.

Ava shook her head. "Henri and Enzo will be back any minute. They need you to help them navigate their way through the church."

Marina bit her upper lip. "I'll never forgive myself if something happens to Apple."

Ava stared at Marina. It was an odd thing for her to say.

Marina took an unlit cigarette out of her pocket and put it between her lips.

Ava ran down the steps and dashed to the right of the church. A pedestrian passageway ran along the side of the church. It swung right and gave onto the rue des Pyramides. Stepping back, Ava looked up at the stained glass windows in the church.

They were dark.

Maybe Laura and Apple hadn't come here. Maybe Marina and Enzo were wrong about the painting being hidden in the church.

Then Ava saw something.

At first, it was the smallest flicker of light on a stained glass window. Squinting, Ava waited. For a brief instant, she wondered if she had imagined the light. Then there was more flickering light. It was barely perceptible. The faint light bounced from window to window. It moved toward the far end of the church.

Someone was inside.

It had to be Laura and Apple.

Loud footsteps echoed on the pavement. Someone was coming from the rue des Pyramides. Ava ducked into the doorway of the building and peered out into the semi-darkness.

Marc Jardin appeared. A man on a mission, he ran toward a side door and pushed his way through the plants that blocked it, knocking pots over as he moved. Ava inched forward. She watched him plunge his hand into a huge terracotta pot that had an olive tree growing out of it. He pulled something out of the pot and disappeared behind the other plants.

Seconds later, the side door swung open.

Without hesitating, Ava dashed from her hiding place and sprinted toward it. She had to reach it before it slammed shut. Knocking into the plants on the steps, she raced to the door. She managed to catch it just before it closed.

Holding it open, she hesitated.

Should she block it open and go get Marina?

Standing there, Henri's words ran through her mind. *If they didn't stop Laura, she would kill Apple.*

Having tried to kill Marc once, Ava doubted that Laura would hesitate to kill him a second time.

There was no time to get Marina. Ava had to act now if she wanted to save Apple and Marc. Pulling the door open wider, Ava stepped inside.

The church was dark and silent. It was an oppressive silence that hung heavy in the air.

Ava stood in the dark and let her eyes adjust to it.

Marc was somewhere nearby.

But Marc knew the church. He had known about the hidden key.

Ava closed her eyes and tried to remember the layout of the church from the memorial service.

The St. Roch Church was an enormous Baroque church. In the central section, there was altar after altar. The sacristy was on the opposite side of the church.

Suddenly, light moved across the stone pillars at the far end of the church. Ava remembered that the back section of the church had been closed to the public during the memorial service.

George must have worked there.

And that's where she would find Laura and Apple.

Ava moved slowly through the darkness. She didn't want to knock anything over and alert the others to her presence.

There was another flicker of light ahead of her. It was extinguished immediately.

As it was closer than the first light, Ava guessed that it was Marc.

She waited.

After a few seconds, there was another flicker of light. Again, it was extinguished immediately.

Ava began to follow it.

As she moved, the silence in the church grew louder and louder. Danger hung in the air.

As she approached the back of the church, she heard footsteps and whispered voices coming toward her. She jumped behind a pillar and hid.

Laura and Apple strode out of the back of the church, each holding a candlestick with a lit candle in it.

"The painting is here," Apple told Laura. "I can feel it."

"Are you sure it's not in the Beehive?" Laura asked, worried.

Apple shook her head. "After George's death, I looked everywhere. I didn't find a painting. But then I wasn't looking for a Cranach."

Laura followed Apple through the dark cavernous church.

Ava crept out of her hiding spot, trying to keep them in sight.

The two women were now walking down the far side of the church. They stopped at each side altar and held their candlesticks high as Apple examined the paintings on each altar.

Keeping low, Ava followed them from her side of the church. Several times, she spotted movement directly behind Apple and Laura.

It had to be Marc.

The two women didn't appear to notice the movement.

As she and Apple advanced through the church, Laura became more and more agitated. "Maybe we should search the back room again," she said as Apple continued to examine the paintings in the church.

Apple shook her head. "It's not there. We already looked. George hid it in the church. He once joked that the best place to hide something was in plain sight."

As Apple spoke, her eyes caught sight of something on a pillar.

"What is it, Apple?" Laura asked, picking up on the change in the woman's behavior.

"It's there," Apple said, pointing to a painting that was hanging high up on a stone pillar.

The women walked over to the painting. As Apple studied it, Laura held her candlestick high in the air, lighting it.

"That's not the Cranach," Laura said.

Frowning, Apple eyed the area around them. She strode over to the altar in the center of the church and dragged a heavy candelabrum over to the painting. She placed it at the bottom of the painting and lit the candles.

From her hiding spot, Ava watched, terrified.

The minute they found the Cranach, Laura would kill Apple.

Apple pointed at the painting. "This was the painting George finished before his death. The original disappeared during the French Revolution. George used descriptions from church and tax records to recreate it. That's how we painted it."

"You painted it together?" Laura asked.

Apple smiled sadly. "That was our sacred bond. But I didn't paint the Cranachs. If George painted Cranachs, he did them on his own." Frowning, Apple stared at the painting from below. "I need to climb up there."

Laura put her candlestick down. She picked up a chair and carried it over to the painting.

Apple climbed up on it. She was still too low to reach the painting. "We need to find something to lift the chair."

They looked around the church.

"The planter," Laura said, pointing at a large wooden planter with a palm tree in it that stood next to a side altar.

Laura and Apple pulled the wooden planter over to the painting. It made a loud screeching noise as it moved across the stone floor.

Apple put the chair on top of the planter. The chair wobbled. "Hold it for me."

Laura held the chair as Apple climbed up on it.

Apple's hand now reached the bottom of the painting. Standing on her toes, she ran her hand under the painting's right corner. "Nothing here."

She jumped down. She and Laura dragged the planter and the chair to the other side of the painting. As Apple climbed up on the chair, it tipped over. Apple fell. Laura helped her up.

"Are you hurt?" Laura asked.

Apple rubbed her shoulder. "I'm fine."

As Laura steadied the chair, Apple climbed up on it and ran her hand under the left side of the painting.

"Is there anything there?" Laura asked.

"No," Apple said. She continued to move her hand. "Wait. I can feel something." She stood on her toes and pulled something out from behind the painting. Clutching it in her hand, she climbed down.

"Is it the Cranach?" Laura asked, her voice rising with excitement.

Moving closer to the light of the large candelabrum, Apple held out a small package covered in oilcloth. She unwrapped it.

Sensing the tension rise, Ava crept into the center of the church to get closer to the two women. She could feel Marc moving toward them.

As her heart beat faster, a last doubt swept over Ava. *What if Marc was behind everything?*

Marc could have killed Nicolas for money. When he

didn't get any, he created a false blackmail story to get the painting from George. Just when he was about to succeed, George suspected him. When George went to the Louvre to meet someone from London, Marc followed him there and killed him. Marc then used the same story to try and get the painting from Laura. Faking his own death was part of an elaborate plot. He would get the painting and disappear. And now he was in the St. Roch Church about to carry out his plan. He had already murdered two people. What would two more matter?

Terrified, Ava froze. Unsure of what to do, she looked from Laura to Apple.

Instantly, she knew she was wrong.

The Marc who had been whimpering in George's studio an hour earlier wasn't capable of such subterfuge...

But Laura was.

Hadn't Leo Montaigne said that she was very intelligent?

Looking up, she saw Laura raise her candlestick in the air and swing it at Apple's head.

"Watch out!" Ava shouted as she began to run.

Apple ducked.

With a roar, Marc leapt out from his hiding place and tackled Laura. Her candlestick clattered noisily to the ground. The two rolled on the floor in a death grip. Ava dashed over and pushed a confused Apple out of the way.

Laura was now on top of Marc and was strangling him. Marc was gasping for air.

Ava grabbed Apple's candlestick and swung it at Laura's head. It missed it by inches.

Startled, Laura released Marc. With a bound, she jumped up and ran toward the exit as the church lights went on. She pushed past Henri, Marina, Enzo and Father Philippe. She ran out of the church.

"Laura!" Enzo shouted as he sprinted after her with Marina on his heels.

Henri and Father Philippe hurried through the church toward Marc, Apple and Ava.

Father Philippe knelt over Marc who was sprawled on the floor. He helped him to sit up.

"How do you feel?" Henri asked, crouching down next to Marc.

"Pretty good for a dead man," Marc said in a vain attempt at humor.

There was sound of a violent collision outside the church. It was followed by shouts and screams.

White-faced, Marina appeared at the back of the church. She walked toward the others in a daze.

"Laura's dead. A motorcycle knocked her into a car. Enzo's staying with her," Marina said as she sank down onto a chair, overwhelmed by all that had happened.

Ava strode over to Apple who was sitting on the ground in shock. "Are you OK?"

Clutching the canvas, Apple shook her head, unable to speak.

Henri came over and helped Apple to her feet. She handed the package to Henri who unwrapped it.

"So this is the famous *Hares and Hunters*," Henri said as he examined the painting. "George was very talented."

Stunned, Apple studied the painting. "George was a genius."

Ava walked over to Henri who handed her the painting. A shiver ran through her when she saw it.

The vitality that the drawings in the sketchbook possessed were magnified a thousand times on the canvas. The painting was alive!

Ava wrapped it up carefully and handed it back to Henri.

"I suggest you leave through the side door," Father Philippe said as the sound of sirens filled the church.

Leaning against Henri, Apple walked slowly to the door. Marc came over and joined them.

Marina looked up at Ava. "What are we going to do about Laura?"

Father Philippe made the sign of the cross. "There is nothing you can do. She's in God's hands now."

CHAPTER 21

The Marais neighborhood was in the throes of a hangover.
After the all night party of the night before, a quiet lull hung
over the neighborhood. Nowhere was the lull more
noticeable than at the Beehive.

The front door was locked and its shutters were closed.
As Ava pulled her *Velib'* share bike into the bike station to
return it, three phrases ran through her mind, over and over
again...

*The killer had been caught. Divine retribution had taken place.
Life would go on.*

Ava was too tired to be excited or elated about what had
happened. She and Henri had caught George's killer, Laura
Gossal. Laura had probably killed Nicolas Delavine or, at the

very least, didn't help him as he lay dying in his apartment. If Ava and Marc had not been in the church, Apple would be dead, too. If Ava hadn't swung the candlestick at Laura, Marc might also be dead. Laura was so clever that she probably would have pinned everything on Apple.

But now that Laura was dead, they'd never know the whole truth. To a budding sleuth like Ava, that was frustrating.

"Ava!" Henri shouted as he stepped out of a taxi.

Ava turned just as a woman got out of the taxi behind him. It was her *doppelganger*, her look alike.

Henri carried out the introductions. "Ava Sext, this is Annabelle Windsor."

The two women stared at each other for an eternity.

Annabelle was a beautiful woman in her late forties. Her skin was perfect, and her long hair hung down her back. She was wearing simple black trousers, a grey sweater and black flats with silver studs.

Ava was well aware that her face was red from her bike ride and that her hair was pulled back in a makeshift chignon. She was happy that she was wearing her favorite blue skirt and simple black top that looked perfect with anything. She was even happier that she had put on her favorite red lipstick that gave her a "*bonne mine*", a healthy glow. Still, if this were a beauty contest, Annabelle won hands down.

Annabelle broke the silence and smiled at Ava. "We've met twice before if I'm not mistaken."

Henri looked from one woman to the other. "The resemblance is remarkable. I can see where George might have gotten confused."

"He hadn't seen me since our divorce," Annabelle said.

Ava's eyebrows shot up.

Annabelle smiled at her. "We met in art school, got married and divorced in that order. Our divorce has lasted much longer than our very brief and foolish marriage."

"Annabelle is a curator who organizes shows at different British museums," Henri explained.

Annabelle put her finger up to her lips. "I'd rather that people didn't know that."

"So you were the person George was meeting?" Ava asked, trying to understand the woman's role in everything.

Annabelle nodded. "He called me out of the blue. First, it was to set up an association with me as the administrator. It was only later he told me about his Cranach problem. Of course, I'd heard about the Cranach controversy. When the painting was declared authentic, it was a relief to everyone in the museum world."

Ava frowned. "I don't understand. Wouldn't a museum want to know if they had purchased a fake?"

Annabelle laughed. "After they bought the painting?

Absolutely not. It's almost impossible for a museum to raise money to acquire new art today. With every millionaire and billionaire trying to outbid the other for the most minor paintings, prices have soared so high that museums are crowded out of the market. For the Cranach, the museum begged, borrowed and stole to get the money to buy it. Can you imagine what would have happened to future fundraising if it had been declared a fake?"

"But it is a fake," Ava protested, confused.

Annabelle shook her head. "A panel of experts has declared the painting authentic. Therefore, it is authentic. Who are we to question the experts? If museums started to take down paintings that might be fakes, the walls of most major museums would be half-empty."

Henri looked at his watch. "We need to get going. The others are waiting for us." He glanced at Ava. "I told Annabelle everything that happened."

Annabelle looked sad. "I'll miss George. I hadn't seen or heard from him in over twenty years... But once you met him, he stayed with you."

"George Starr will always be alive," Ava said with conviction.

They knocked on the door to the Beehive. A pale Marina let them in. She did a double-take when she saw the resemblance between Annabelle and Ava. Henri introduced everyone.

"How are you?" Henri asked Marina.

"Stunned. I can't wrap my mind around that fact that Laura killed George and Nicolas. But then we'll never know the truth. The police told Enzo that Laura died immediately. Let's go into the sitting room," she said with a wave of her hand.

The wine and plastic cups from the night before were gone. A teapot was on the table. Mismatched porcelain cups were next to it.

"English breakfast tea. The kitchen is filled with it. Some habits George never lost," Marina explained as she poured tea for everyone.

The Cranach was on the fireplace mantle.

Hares and Hunters was in all its glory.

Annabelle and Ava walked up to it.

The painting was full of life. A hare had cornered a hunter at the top of a tree. Elsewhere, two hares were carrying a hunter bound to a stick. A blazing fire with a spit was in the foreground.

"This is wonderful!" Annabelle said as her eyes lit up in admiration.

Ava nodded. It was more than wonderful, it was magical.

Apple entered the room. Despite her ordeal the night before, she was full of energy.

"How are you?" Ava asked, concerned.

"Shaken, but I'm happy at the same time."

"Happy?" Ava repeated, confused.

Apple strode over to the painting. "This is the proof that George was a great artist. He painted it on his own."

Ava glanced at Henri who once again carried out the introductions.

When Apple learned that Annabelle was George's ex-wife, she paled. "He never mentioned you."

With a warm smile on her face, Annabelle took Apple's arm. "That's because George lived in the present. You were his present."

"Was," Apple said.

"You have the Beehive. You'll carry on George's work. He wanted it to continue," Annabelle said.

"If we get the money," Enzo said as he entered the room with Marc.

Annabelle turned to everyone. "George contacted me because he wanted to sell *Hares and Hunters*. He wanted to buy the Beehive and help Marc pay his blackmailer. When I arrived at the Louvre that day, he was already dead."

"Killed by Laura who must have been my blackmailer," Marc said bitterly.

Marina was confused. She looked from Annabelle to Henri. "If Annabelle was the person meeting George, then how did you and Ava get involved?"

"Just by chance," Ava answered. "We were in the café, and George spoke to us before he died."

"He must have confused Ava with Annabelle as he hadn't seen her in over twenty years," Henri added.

Enzo moved his eyes from Ava to Annabelle. "I can see where he'd get confused. The resemblance is astounding." Suddenly, Enzo broke down. "I was at the Louvre that morning. I saw you, Apple. I was afraid you'd killed him," Enzo confessed.

Apple was shocked. "How could you imagine such a thing?"

"I'm sorry," Enzo said.

Henri walked to the center of the room and looked from one person to the other. "The question you all have to answer is do you want to sell the painting. Annabelle has a buyer, a discreet buyer. The proceeds will go to the Beehive. There will also be a fund to renovate the building and pay the taxes."

"I agree," Marina said without the slightest hesitation.

Marc nodded. "Count me in."

Enzo eyed Apple. "Have you changed your mind?"

Apple's eyes filled with tears. "Yes. It was George's painting. If he wanted to sell it, it's not for me to say no. I won't be staying here though. Last night in church, I decided to go back to the south of France and paint. Seeing the Cranach that George had painted was a sign. I intend to stop doing digital art and return to my first love, painting. For that, I need light."

"Then who will run the Beehive?" Ava asked.

"I'm not going anywhere," Marina said.

Marc looked at everyone, sheepish. "I may not be a good artist, but I'll try and be a better teacher."

Distraught, Enzo stared at Apple. "You're really leaving?"

Apple nodded. "Nice isn't far from Paris. With the fast train, you can be there in a few hours."

A cloud passed over Marina's face. "It's wrong that Laura got away with murder."

"She didn't. She's dead," Henri said. "That seems a severe enough punishment to me."

There was a knock at the front door. Enzo rose and opened it. He ushered Leo Montaigne into the room. Once again, Henri carried out the introductions. When Leo saw Annabelle, he recognized her immediately.

"I was going to offer my services, but if you're here, the painting is in good hands," Leo said to Annabelle. "Where is it?"

Henri waved his hand toward the fireplace. Without a word, Leo walked over to the painting and studied it. A huge smile appeared on his face. "It's glorious. I can see where art lovers would do anything for art. I tried to buy the Cranach drawings that George based this on. It was sold to another bidder who kept bidding it up. You wouldn't know who that was Henri?"

Henri smiled. "I might. I might even sell it to you if the price is right."

Leo burst out laughing. "I should have known not to try and outsmart a notary."

All at once, Ava frowned. "Who broke into my apartment?"

Enzo raised his hand. "I did. I was worried that you'd seen Apple at the Louvre. I wanted to know who you were. I checked out the phone number you gave Marina. I found the address. I knew you were at the concert so I went there and broke in. How did I get in? I'd worked as a locksmith as a student. But you made it easy for me. The door was slammed closed but not locked. After I saw the apartment, I wasn't worried about you."

"Why not?" Ava asked, puzzled.

"You had a fabulous collection of 60s rock albums. Anyone who had a collection like that can't be all bad. I also saw a photo of an older man. I assumed you liked mature men and had had a fling with George. You scared the life out of me when you shouted!" Enzo admitted.

"The break-in at the gallery wasn't you?" Ava asked.

Enzo shook his head. "No."

"It wasn't me," Marc added.

"The only person who said there was a break-in was Laura. She probably made it up," Henri said.

Marina stood up and poured everyone more tea. Halfway around the room, the teapot was empty. "I'll make some more."

"Ava and I will help you," Henri said, rising to his feet.

In the kitchen, Marina was silent and lost in thought.

Henri handed her a cloth bag. "I have something that's yours."

Marina took the bag without a word and looked inside it. The sketchbook of *Hares and Hunters* was in it. "How do you know it's mine?"

"For the same reason I know that George didn't paint *Hares and Hunters*, you did."

Marina fell silent.

"Why didn't you tell Apple?" Ava asked.

Marina sighed. "Because she needs to believe George painted it to move on with her life."

"What you painted is fabulous," Ava protested.

"It is fabulous. I restore art. I have to get into the psyche of an artist. When I helped George with the first Cranach, I became fascinated with the idea of recreating a painting from scratch. George always said that everyone is an artist. This was my chance to be one. I did it. That's enough."

Ava was puzzled. "Won't you be sorry to see the painting sold?"

Marina shook her head. "It will always be with me. I did it. It was a challenge. I painted *Hares and Hunters*. In forty or fifty years, the painting will be "discovered" and will hang in a museum. Who could ask for more?"

EPILOGUE

"So Laura killed Nicolas Delavine..." Benji said.

"We don't know that. We just suspect that she did. But Laura used the death to shake Marc down to try and get the painting from George after he refused to give it to her," Ava said as she shifted the phone from one hand to another while balancing a cup of tea. "With George dead, Laura believed that she could get her hands on the painting and sell it."

"Weren't they seeing each other?"

"Don't forget that George was very fickle in love," Ava said.

Benji sighed. "Henri was right as usual. Money is behind everything in France."

"You're forgetting love!" Ava added.

Benji paused. "You mean Apple?"

"Yes. Apple loved George. She helped him paint his paintings…"

"Some of which must have been sold to support his lifestyle," Benji said.

"Probably. Although she never spoke about that. Apple could accept the other women. But when she learned that there was a painting she hadn't been involved in, she felt that the sacred bond between them had been broken. She followed him to the Louvre. When he fell, she believed that she had so spooked him that it was her fault," Ava explained.

"Who knows? Maybe if Laura hadn't killed George, Apple would have killed him," Benji said. "Apple agreed to sell the painting in the end?"

"Yes, in homage to George's talent. Everything that happened freed her. She's going back to the south of France to paint."

"Annabelle Windsor, your double, is going to sell the fake?" Benji asked.

"Please don't use the word fake. The painting is of "unknown provenance". If Lucas Cranach the Elder were alive today, he'd be delighted by it. It's a marvelous painting," Ava said.

"What are you going to do now that the case is solved?"

Benji asked in a worried tone.

"If you're implying that I'll be out trolling through Paris for another crime to solve, you're mistaken. I'm taking a drawing class."

There was a long silence on the other end of the phone.

"Not everyone is an artist, Ava," Benji said.

"But some people are. I won't know until I try," Ava replied.

The doorbell rang. Ava rose to her feet.

"I've got to go. The pizza deliveryman is here," Ava said.

"For the neighbor?" Benji asked.

"For me. If the two of you Frenchies can eat pineapple pizza, I can, too. *When in France...*"

Benji burst out laughing.

PREVIEW OF "DEATH ON THE SEINE"

Some days were good. Some days were great. And then there was the rarest day of all -- the perfect day.

For Ava Sext, it was a perfect day.

It was a beautiful day in May.

The sky was blue, the birds were singing and pale green shoots were appearing on the barren branches of the silver-barked trees that lined the Seine River.

Most importantly of all, this perfect day was taking place in Paris.

Smiling broadly, Ava strode down the rue des Saints-Pères on Paris's left bank. Spine straight, head high, she breathed in deeply, content to be basking in the early morning sunshine. In any city of the world, people would be delighted by the weather. But in Paris, a city of grey skies and rain-swept monuments, a beautiful day in May was so unexpected that both Parisians and tourists, as startled, as they were ecstatic, were out in force.

It was only 9 A.M., but the streets were already full of people rollerblading, biking, walking, jogging, or, this being Paris, the city of love, walking hand in hand.

While not in love, no one was more ecstatic than Ava as she hurried to the Quai Malaquais that overlooked the Seine River, for she was going to paradise.

She had only lived in Paris for six months, but her past life was already a distant memory. She had exchanged London's dark skies and rainy days for Paris's dark skies and rainy days... But anyone who knew anything would tell you that they weren't the same. Parisian dark skies were infinitely more poetic. If Ava were a painter, she would pull out an easel and a palette of blacks and grays to capture Paris on one of those poetic rainy days. But she wasn't a painter. She would have to leave that to someone else.

Passing by an upscale antique store, Ava slowed and studied her Parisian "look" in its large plate glass window. Living in Paris had not only changed the way she felt and thought... she often found herself feeling French at the oddest times. It had also changed her external appearance. Her colorful, quirky London style had given way to a more polished look.

Today, she was dressed in her new uniform of slim black jeans and a well-cut white T-shirt. A green leopard print scarf snaked around her neck. Her long, shiny dark hair was pushed behind her ears. Her heart-shaped face was makeup free except for a touch of mascara and bright red lipstick.

In the six months she had been in France, the "must-wear" lipstick color had gone from a gothic-looking purplish black over the Christmas holidays to a pale barely-there touch of pink in early spring, only to come crashing back to the bright fire-engine red color that Ava now had on her lip. As she eyed the tall 27-year-old reed-thin woman who stared back at her from the store window, she had to admit she looked very "chic".

With a smile of approval, she turned, crossed the street and hurried down it, slowing only when she passed by Café Zola. On its outside terrace, a waiter in his forties was setting up tables for the inevitable crowd that would soon appear on such a glorious day. He was wearing a white shirt, black vest and a long, old-fashioned white apron -- the uniform of a traditional Paris waiter,

"Morning, Gerard," Ava said with a light wave.

Gerard lifted his eyebrows in gruff recognition of the pretty woman passing by but continued to place silverware on the tables without a word.

Unperturbed by his silence, Ava continued on her way.

The famous Parisian reserve had taken some getting used to. In London, people were always willing to chat or give their opinion to complete strangers. Whereas the French had an odd habit of speaking when you least expected it and not speaking when you did.

It made no sense at all to Ava. But some things just were. "*C'est la vie,*" as the French would say… That's life.

Looking left to see if any cars were coming down the one-way street, Ava stepped off the sidewalk and headed to the pedestrian island, lost in her thoughts about life in France.

A tinny ringing sound pulled her from her reverie.

Her inner survival instinct told her to jump. As she leapt forward, a cyclist raced by, going the wrong way down the one-way street. Shaken, she stood up, brushed herself off and watched him ride away.

Several pithy insults were on the tip of her tongue, but she stopped herself. It was an exceptionally beautiful day. Paradise was a few steps away. Why ruin it by screaming at a madman on a bike?

Be generous. Be loving… she repeated in a mantra that was definitely not Ava-like.

But this was Paris in May.

It was time for change. It was time for a new Ava.

She slowed next to the gigantic marble statue of a woman with a sword that stood on a triangle of land between the two sides of the street. She eyed it. The woman was an allegory of the French Republic. She and her sword were announcing to the world that they were ready for anything.

Ava frowned.

Maybe she needed what the statue had... that very definite "don't mess with me" attitude. Would the cyclist have rung his bell and tried to mow the statue down if it had suddenly come to life and crossed the street?

Of course not.

The statue would have beheaded the cyclist with one swift swing of her sword.

Cheered by the thought, Ava looked right and left before crossing the next street, a busy thoroughfare. She bolted across car lanes, bus lanes and bike lanes to reach her destination: the 8.60 meters of bottle-green wooden boxes that were perched on a stone wall overlooking the Seine River below.

Paradise.

With a double twist of her key, Ava unlocked the heavy metal padlocks that secured the bottle-green boxes, one by one. When she unlocked the last lock, she flung the wooden tops back revealing rows and rows of used books in French and

English.

She ran her hands over their bindings and closed her eyes, then breathed in deeply. It was a ritual she had performed every morning since the green boxes had become hers.

The books in the boxes had a special odor that came from being stored next to the Seine. Ava liked to imagine that it was a secret scent made up of all the places that the passing boats on the river below had been to and the adventures they had had. Just as she liked to believe that in the past six months she had learned to like adventure, at least a little...

After all, she was now living in Paris.

Her gaze turned to the license taped inside the first green box. The license was written in French and had several official stamps on it. It stated that the city of Paris authorized Ava Sext to run this little part of paradise.

Ava was a "*bouquinist*": a bookseller that sold used books out of the green boxes that lined the Seine River in the center of Paris. Since 1859, concessions to the boxes that ran from the Pont Marie to the Quai de Louvre and from the Quai de la Tournelle to the Quai Voltaire had been granted by the city of Paris to a lucky few.

Ava grabbed a green and white striped folding lawn chair off the top of the books, carried it over to a tall tree and unfolded it. If the green boxes were her kingdom, her folding chair was the throne from which she reigned. From it, she could see the Tuileries Garden and the Louvre Museum on the opposite bank. Further down the river, the tall spires of a cathedral soared high in the air. Like Quasimodo, Ava saw Notre Dame every day, and she didn't even have to ring any bells to do so.

If she leaned against the stone wall behind her stand, she could watch the *"Bateaux Mouches"*, the flat-bottomed glass-topped tourist boats, drift by on the water below as they made their runs up and down the river.

She wasn't exaggerating when she told people that she worked in paradise.

Her book stand was paradise... paradise on earth.

Humming a cheerful tune that she made up as she went along, she hung a vintage rock concert poster on the stone wall, unfolded a rickety metal postcard stand and stood it up. She put a piece of folded paper under one of its wobbly legs to stabilize it. She then strung copies of turn-of-the-century engravings across the top of her stand. They made paradise look very colorful indeed.

Last of all, she rearranged the small assortment of bric-a-brac that her stand sold, items that the French and tourists loved as much as the books. This morning, there were two black cat vases, a set of souvenir cups from the south of France, a metal cobra candlestick that looked like it had come from an Arab bazaar in North Africa and a pair of blue porcelain rabbit salt and pepper shakers.

Ava picked the rabbits up and held one in each hand. "I'll be sad to see you two leave," she told them. Unsurprisingly, the rabbits remained silent.

For a brief instant, she thought of keeping them for herself. However, she put them back with regret as she remembered the first rule of a *"bouquinist"*: Once something was in your stand, you sold it... No exceptions.

Not ready to see the rabbits leave, she moved the pair to the back of the box and hid them behind a cracked crystal ball.

With a sense of contentment that mirrored the sunlight dancing off the river below, she stepped back and gazed approvingly at her stand.

It was now officially open and ready for business.

It was a perfect day in paradise... A day where everything would go according to some celestial plan. A day where nothing could possibly go wrong. However, even Ava, with her over-active imagination, couldn't have imagined that she would meet a dead man before lunch and that he would walk away.

ABOUT THE BOOK

Evan's *Paris Booksellers Mysteries* are light-hearted cozy mysteries that plunge you into the joys and tribulations of living in Paris, where food, wine and crime make life worth living… along with a book or two.

Evan also writes the *Isa Floris* thrillers that blend together far-flung locations, ancient secrets and fast-paced action in an intriguing mix of fact and fiction aimed at keeping you on the edge of your seat.

Find out more about Evan Hirst's books at

www.evanhirst.com

Made in the USA
Middletown, DE
05 May 2019